"Why in hell do I want you?"

he asked quietly.

"Answer me. Is it because you're beautiful? Is it because you smell so good? Is it because I want to unbraid your hair and spread it on my belly?"

She moved away to stand by the window. Her shoulders trembled, and he cursed himself for saying as much as he had.

"Look," Keely began, turning to face him. "I have thirty days to prove I can handle things here. I know you only came out of obligation to my father, and I don't want to interfere in your life. So why don't you go? I should be able to get someone else in a couple of days."

"No."

"No?"

"I'm here, and I intend to stay."

"And what about these, uh, feelings between us?"

"Can you keep your hands off me?"

Her chin came up. "Of course I can."

"Then all we need to worry about is me."

Dear Reader:

As usual, we've gathered the cream of the crop for you this month in Silhouette Intimate Moments. Start off with Beverly Sommers and the first book in a terrific new trilogy, "Friends for Life." In *Accused* she tells the story of Jack Quintana, a man accused of a murder he didn't commit. His defender is Anne Larkin, a woman whose memories of Jack are less than fond. As they work together to clear his name, however, they discover that love isn't necessarily the most logical of emotions. In the next two months, look for *Betrayed* and *Corrupted*, the stories of Anne's friends Bolivia and Sandy. These three really are *friends for life*.

Also this month, Heather Graham Pozzessere returns with *A Perilous Eden*, a story of terror on the high seas and passion under the hot Caribbean sun. It's an adventure not to be missed. Lee Magner brings you *Sutter's Wife*, the story of a make-believe marriage that quickly becomes the real thing. Finish the month with new author Dee Holmes and *Black Horse Island*, a stunning debut performance from a writer to watch.

In coming months, look for new books by Emilie Richards, Barbara Faith, Marilyn Pappano and Jennifer Greene, not to mention fall treats from, among others, Linda Howard, Kathleen Korbel and Patricia Gardner Evans. Something great is always happening at Silhouette Intimate Moments.

Leslie J. Wainger
Senior Editor

Black Horse Island

DEE HOLMES

Silhouette Intimate Moments

Published by Silhouette Books New York

America's Publisher of Contemporary Romance

SILHOUETTE BOOKS
300 East 42nd St., New York, N.Y. 10017

ISBN: 0-373-07327-5

First Silhouette Books printing March 1990

Printed in the U.S.A.

DEE HOLMES

would love to tell her readers about her exciting trips to Europe or that she has mastered a dozen languages. But the truth is that traveling isn't her thing, and she flunked French twice. Perhaps because of a military background where she was uprooted so much, Dee married a permanent civilian.

Dee is an obsessive reader who started writing casually, only to discover that "writing is hard! And writing a publishable book is even harder." She has since become involved in her local RWA chapter, and says that she loves to write about "relationships between two people who are about to fall in love, but they don't know how exciting it is going to be for them."

To Patricia Rorie
for the "long-distance" friendship
and the encouragement that never quit.

To Eileen Fallon,
who found the wheat in the chaff.

And to Reinier...
who always believed.

Chapter 1

Jed came home from work and found her sitting cross-legged in the middle of his bed. She wore the biggest glasses he'd ever seen. Across her lap lay his scrapbook. Carefully, she turned the pages. Through the open window came a stew pot of inner-city smells and sounds thickened by the July heat. If she were anyone else, Jed thought, he would have given every swearword he knew an additional definition.

"Jed Corey?" she asked when she saw him, as if it were her apartment and he the intruder.

Her pink cotton shirt was big enough to circle her three times. Her breasts were hidden well enough to frustrate a casual observer. Her white jeans, by contrast, were tight. She'd taken off sandals that were more strap than substance, and they lay on the floor as though putting her shoes under a man's bed didn't concern her. His sheets were rumpled under her bare feet. A bandage covered her left big toe. Skinny and scabby, he remembered her looking, but despite the long single brown braid that curled over her shoulder, Keely Lockwood was all grown-up.

Jed leaned against the doorframe. Her glasses fascinated him; he wondered why she didn't wear contact lenses.

"Didn't the Judge ever teach you breaking and entering is against the law?" he asked.

For a moment surprise crossed her face, making her look vulnerable. "You know who I am." He liked her voice. It had a soft huskiness that suggested innocence.

Keely glanced down at the scrapbook page. A picture of herself with Seth and two people from the Board was the last entry. It was a grainy newsprint photo that had appeared in the *Providence Journal* the week before, announcing the reopening of Black Horse Island. In the photo she was wearing what she called her charm-the-bureaucrats outfit. Blue linen suit, straw hat, white pumps and only enough gold to avoid being ostentatious.

"The shoes were killing me." She grinned at him and wiggled her toes.

Jed guessed she probably wore shoes only when necessary. Barefoot and pregnant slipped into his thoughts, and he escorted the image right back out again.

"I'm flattered you recognized me," she said, closing the scrapbook but keeping her hands on the top. "Your landlord let me in."

Jed cocked an eyebrow at that. "Oakes? No way. Oakes wouldn't let Joe Frazier in here."

She lifted a glass of whiskey from somewhere in the depths of her shirt and took a swallow. He waited for the wince, the grimace, for her eyes to blink and water.

No wince, no grimace, not even a pause between sips. She was enjoying this.

Jed wasn't. The Judge's daughter in his bed, even innocently, was enough to disturb him. But more unsettling was the slice of pure pleasure he felt at the possibility of keeping her there.

She moistened her lips and used the glass to push up her spectacles. "I've never met a man who kept a scrapbook."

He'd never met a woman who looked at his scrapbook. "How did you get in here?"

"I paid your rent."

He scowled and straightened, then closed the door very softly. The click beat between them. From outside came the smell of bus exhaust and the rattling roll of a skateboard.

He crossed the room with long strides, his heavy boots light on the floor. The faint odor of varnish clung to him as he walked into the bathroom. He returned with a roll of bills wrapped in a rubber band, and picked up her handbag.

It was a mass of flaps and fringe, pine colored and with a soft texture that felt the way her skin looked. For an unguarded moment, he wanted to lift her up and press her in to him. He was closer to her now, and her scent lay against him light and fresh like violets after a summer rain.

He took a single step back to clear his head. He flipped back the center flap of her purse. The long metal object resting on a bag of candy gleamed like an old enemy, reminding him of a painful memory—a twenty-two-year-old scar that carved an ugly six-inch path down his belly.

"I thought women carried Mace and whistles," he said, handling the switchblade as though it had been born in his hand. The handle was carved and wrapped in leather. He snapped it open. The blade glistened in the hot afternoon light. It was expensive, precise—and deadly.

"Goes to show you don't know much about women," she replied with a decided lack of sarcasm. She sounded as if she'd discovered something about him that he didn't want to think about.

"And I like it that way." He closed the knife and dropped it into the handbag. It hit the hard candies with a heavy crunch. He tossed the roll of bills on top, shoved the handbag at her and retrieved the scrapbook.

He held the book, Keely thought, as if it contained his life. For an instant, she wondered if he'd ever possessed a woman with that degree of protective intensity.

He laid the scrapbook on the card table where she'd found it, amid unopened mail, three empty beer cans, a set of carving tools and a tiny wooden tiger.

Finely detailed, the tiger's stripes were meticulously carved and shaped into the wood. She was curious about the tiger. Had he carved it? she wondered. Was he a man who caressed a switchblade and carved toys with the same touch?

Jed Corey, she decided as she watched him, moved like a tiger, with a lean tight motion that wasn't calculated or practiced. His jeans were worn and gray in intimate places. His blue chambray shirt was wrinkled, the sleeves rolled up above his elbows. His arms were tanned and muscled. Wood shavings clung to the dark hairs. He wore no wristwatch, and she knew rings would be as foreign to him as a ruffled shirt.

His face wasn't handsome. His cheeks were too hollow. His nose had been broken. On anyone else the face lines would be called laugh lines; on Jed they were barren, stark and etched like jagged webs. She'd been aware of that when he held the knife.

His eyes were gray smoke with the barest hint of silver around the pupils. They were unreadable, distant, yet Keely had seen them a million times—in the kids on the street, in the broken homes, in the cry for help. Her father had seen that unreadable coldness in Jed Corey when he was sixteen.

This Jed Corey was no kid.

He opened the door as quietly as he'd closed it earlier.

"Sorry you have to leave," he said, using the words her mother uttered when a dinner guest had to depart after a pleasant visit, but with none of the regret.

Keely remained in the middle of the bed. "If you had the money, why didn't you pay your rent?"

His eyes were direct, unblinking. "I'm a deadbeat."

He was anything but, and she knew it; not by what he said or the way he dressed, or even the starkness of the apartment, but by his almost unlimited control.

Jed folded his arms and waited.

She didn't move from the bed. The glasses slipped lower on her nose.

Her eyes were a soft spring green; they were too pretty, too curious and too damn confident. He visualized her running barefoot down a sandy beach, unconcerned about sharp stones or broken shells, eager to reach some distant goal, unacquainted with failure.

The glasses were poised on the tip of her nose. Instead of pushing them up, she tipped her head back to stare at him. The pulse in her throat fluttered.

"Macho swagger," she said, undisturbed by his rudeness and his dismissal. "The boys will love you." She pulled her glasses off, fished around in the depths of her purse and came up with a soft leather case, the kind a Girl Scout would make in craft class. She pushed the glasses inside the case and dropped them on top of the switchblade.

Scrambling off the bed, she slung her handbag over her shoulder. With a soft seriousness, she added, "Try to keep it not so blatant. They all think they're Rambos as it is. Seth was right, I have to admit. You're exactly what the Island needs."

At the mention of Seth's name, she was sure she saw a flicker of interest.

"Seth is there," she said quickly, not averse to using her father's old friend and helper as a drawing card. "And of course, the kids. I want you to come with me."

Actually, it was convince Jed or see her father's dream die as silently as he had. Judge Nelson, the chairman of the Children in Crisis board, told her the only way the board would consider her as director of the Island was if she had extra male help. There were other staff members, of course, but they were there for the general functions of the Island. Judge Nelson wanted a man strong enough to handle teenage boys. Seth had pushed hard for Jed Corey. True, he didn't have book education, but he knew street kids. After hours of talking, Judge Nelson and the rest of the board agreed to a thirty-day test period for Keely. She needed Jed Corey.

"You don't need a blue suit, and you don't have to fill out anything in triplicate."

For the first time she saw a hint of a smile.

"Bureaucratic bull," he said.

"Amen."

He unfolded his arms, making himself look curiously exposed. Keely doubted that opening himself, especially to a woman, was a familiar action for him.

His words stole out with a raw reverence. "That was what the Judge always said."

She felt an unexpected welling of tears. "I know. He got fed up with the red tape, too."

"So why has anything changed?"

"I work in the system, counseling mostly, in the Family Services Division. As traitorous as it sounds to my sex, being a woman can be handy at times. Plus, I pulled a few strings."

"That's not what it's called where I come from."

"I was trying to act like a lady."

He arched one eyebrow. "A lady wouldn't have been sitting in a strange man's bed."

"She would have if she wanted something from him."

He chuckled.

"That was a baited comment. Where's the quick comeback?"

"Sorry, I'm fresh out of quickies."

Keely laughed.

He left the door open as though he were protecting her reputation. Silly, she thought, and yet Seth had told her Jed Corey made his own rules.

He picked up the glass she'd been drinking from, and finished the whiskey. Keely felt the liquid sliding in her stomach as if she had swallowed the liquor. A mellow sense of intimacy came over her.

Jed walked to the window, his back to her. He slipped his hands, palms out, into his back pockets. Keely waited, experiencing a nervous uneasiness. Silhouetted against the window, he had assumed a thoughtful stance as though his decision to come to the Island depended on more than her need for him.

"Jed?" She slid her feet into the sandals, reaching down to smooth the bandage under the strap. "When can I expect you? The boys will arrive in a couple of days. We're still getting things ready. Maybe you'd like to come and help." She deliberately didn't make it a question. She wanted to include him, but she knew the reason for his coming would be the kids. "The ferry leaves for the Island at seven tomorrow morning. I could meet you at the dock."

"I'm not going, Keely."

"Not going...?" She blinked as if he'd told her he planned to leap out the window.

He turned around, his hands, still in the back pockets, stretching the front of his jeans, revealing an intimate shape. It brought a sudden increase to her pulse, which she hoped didn't show in her eyes.

"What happened to the feisty lady with the switchblade?"

"This isn't some joke! If you weren't interested, why didn't you say so? For that matter, why didn't you answer my phone calls?" She swung toward the card table and grabbed two unopened letters. She stalked across the room and shoved them at his chest. "Or open your mail? No one leaves their mail unopened."

He trapped her hand against his chest. With his other hand, he removed the barrier of the letters. The chambray shirt lay soft and warm against her palm. One of her fingers slipped under the material where a button was missing. Chest hair brushed her skin, coaxing her finger inside. He didn't pull her close or push her away. His eyes studied her with an almost clinical stare.

He spoke gently, as though calming a frightened dove. "I knew what was in your letters. The newspapers have been carrying stories about the Island since your father died."

The hollows in his cheeks seemed to deepen with each thud of his heart. She felt the beat, steady like him, not excited or out of control. Keely felt herself relax.

Jed, using the lightest of touches, tipped her chin up. He grinned, the lines around his eyes deepening. "Is this where I'm supposed to say I'll come if you sleep with me?"

She wasn't as insulted as she was angry, and some part of her wondered about that. She met his eyes directly. The gray color entwined her like a mysterious fog. Danger beckoned and taunted. Run, Keely, run....

She looked away, then back at him. "You're not my type."

"Good."

She knew any other man would have said, "Oh? And what is your type?" But then Jed Corey wasn't like any man she'd ever met.

She pulled her hand away, felt a disconnection and told herself that was dumb. Coming here had been an even dumber idea. She should have assumed from her ignored letters that he wasn't interested, which would have saved her from all these strange sensations churning inside her.

He didn't move or try to stop her.

She didn't like giving up. Her father wouldn't have given up. She tried a different approach. "I didn't just pick you out of the air, you know. I know you were at the Island when you were sixteen, and I know you were one of Dad's successes. You don't think I just took Seth's word, do you? I hear you're an excellent carpenter, proved by the homes for low-income families you've helped build. I know you work with kids over at St. Mark's Orphanage, kids who have benefited because they can relate to you.'' She took a deep breath. To her surprise, the tips of his ears were red. Jed Corey was embarrassed.

''Keely, I'm not God or some saint. I'm not even very friendly most times. I do what I do. Don't glorify it beyond what it is. There are times when I get down-and-dirty drunk. And on occasion I take a woman to bed with every impure motive you can think of, the primary one being lust.''

Keely glanced at the bed, unable to stop herself from wondering about the kind of woman Jed would seek out for sex. He'd already told her he was glad he wasn't her type. But then, she'd spent little time since her divorce thinking about men of any type.

''Why are you refusing to come? If Dad were alive and he asked you—''

''That's different.''

A sad memory surfaced: her father saying the same thing to her when she was eleven, and she wanted to move back to the Island to be with him, to help him. He'd refused, telling her he didn't want to worry about her; he wanted her always safe and happy. She'd cried and begged, but to no avail. She'd seen the sadness in his eyes, the desire to straddle both worlds—his blood family, and the teenage boys he loved. Boys like Jed.

Keely placed her hand back on Jed's chest, wishing she were the seductive type. If it would have worked, she would have used it. "Why are you refusing when I ask you?"

"Why are you going?"

"Because I think Dad would have wanted me to."

"Did he tell you that? Or ask you?"

She shook her head. "The Island meant more to him than anything." Including his family, she thought. "It stands to reason he would want it to continue."

"Despite your obvious zeal, Keely, it's going to take more than a switchblade and a few pulled strings for that to happen."

"I know that."

He touched her braid, his fingers slowly examining each twist as if it held undiscovered secrets. "Say hello to Seth for me. He's a good man and a good friend."

"You didn't answer my question."

"You wouldn't like the answer."

Possibilities jumped through her mind, but they were clichés. Jed Corey's reason, whatever it was, wouldn't be ordinary. "Tell me," she said, wanting to know, and at the same time bracing herself for what he'd predicted.

"Have you ever heard 'To every thing there is a season? A time to be born, and a time to die'? The Judge was the season for the Island. When he died, the Island died."

She stared at him for a long moment while absorbing the bald finality of his words. No, he was wrong! Black Horse had been her father's dream. Now it was her dream.

"I'm sorry you feel that way," she whispered, her throat tight with disappointment. It would have been better if he'd told her she was crazy. If he'd told her it wasn't any place for a woman. If he'd told her, sorry,

I'm too busy. But his words had a deep, thick sound, and she knew she'd never change his mind.

"Keely?"

She looked back, her hand on the doorknob.

"Your father would be proud of you."

Jed listened to her footsteps going down the stairs, her sandals clacking. She was obviously impatient to put him and her disappointment behind her. The front door slammed. He echoed the sound with his own door. Her violet scent lingered, and he rubbed his shirt where her hand had been.

He moved over to the window and watched her come out from the shadows of the building. Her handbag strap crossed from her right shoulder to her left hip—a purse snatcher's challenge. Finally, he released the breath he'd been holding.

He knew a lot about her—from the pictures in his scrapbook, from his talks with the Judge. A picture of her, at about ten years old, had sat on the Judge's desk at the Island when Jed arrived when he was sixteen.

Twenty years ago, he thought, and the memory remained vivid. Back then, when his life was unfit for a human, he'd believed trouble was a measure of his worth, beer was food, and women were his constitutional right.

The kid in the picture had had scabby knees, gum in her hair and a bunny in her arms. The bunny had a bandage on one leg. The Judge had seen Jed's eyes darting from the thick manila folder that the Rhode Island juvenile system had been compiling since he stole a carton of cigarettes for his ma when he was six, to the picture of the little girl who looked more like a ruffian than a judge's daughter.

Jed had told himself a man like the Judge would dress his daughter in ruffles and ribbons and a say-cheese smile. Yet when the Judge leaned back, looking not at the manila folder but at Keely, his comment had been filled with pride. She had a soft spot for hurt creatures, the Judge had said.

Hurt creatures, Jed thought now as he dragged his hands through his black hair.

After all these years, pain and rejection still lived inside him. From lost years on the street, wandering, feeling angry, looking in department store windows at mannequins with permanent smiles and warm clothes, seeing his own face and hearing the truth. *No one wants you.*

Leave the bitterness, the Judge had told him; that was the path to destruction. But the residue still littered his soul. The Judge, like his daughter, had had a soft spot for hurt creatures.

Jed spread the curtain wider, watching her walk. No, she was mad; her strides were more of a punishment to the sidewalk. Bold, the lady was, and also a little reckless. Maybe somewhat unsure of herself, as evidenced by the tight jeans and the oversize blouse.

A station wagon with Vermont plates, luggage on the roof and two kids in the back seat, pulled over to the curb. The driver leaned out the window and motioned to Keely. He said something, and she pointed in the opposite direction, then made a few hand signals that looked to Jed like directions to England. He grinned.

One of the kids, a girl with blond hair, leaned out the window and showed Keely a doll she was holding. Keely smiled at the child with a warmth Jed knew he saw despite the distance. The image of barefoot and pregnant came to him again, this time with more clarity. Keely

Lockwood would be a natural with kids. She ruffled the girl's hair and stepped back while the station wagon drove away.

Jed heard the door open, but didn't turn around.

"Hey, Jed? Hey, man? How come you been holdin' out on me?"

"Don't bother to knock, Oakes," he said, watching Keely move, her steps on the pavement softer now. She stopped beside a blue car, unlocked the door and slipped inside.

The last time he'd seen the Judge was the day he'd bought that car. Like her determination to continue the Island, Jed wondered if the vehicle was another way to keep herself connected to her father.

He turned around, letting the curtain fall. "Holding out about what?"

Mugsy Oakes gave him a six-tooth smile. Oakes was nearing fifty and paunchy. A former boxer of dubious distinction in his youth, he had a face that bore the results of the quick, hard jabs of his opponents.

"The broad, man."

"Lady, Oakes. She's the Judge's daughter."

"Down here on Clayton Street? Well, ain't that a crock." He hiked up his pants, which rode below his belly. "She bribed me, you know," he said, his tone displaying a mock shock. "What'd she lift? That bankroll you hide? Or your tools? Ain't nothin' else in here worth takin'." Then he added, "'Bout time you got yourself a woman. I worry about you."

"You worry about collecting rent and getting Josephine into your apartment long enough to make a move on her."

Oakes made a garbled sound. "She'll come around," he said with a nod of confidence. "They all do. I mean, how does she resist this mug? I'm just like a friendly old pup.''

While Oakes talked Jed walked into the kitchen and returned with two cold beers. "Josephine likes birds, remember? Why don't you practice cooing instead of barking."

Oakes took the offered can and popped the top. "Very funny. How come you don't buy light beer? Better for my belly." He drank and belched.

Jed dropped into a chair, stretching out his legs in front of him. He rested the beer can on his belt buckle and studied the middle of his bed. Violets still lingered in his senses.

"She's going to be director at Black Horse," Jed said.

"She's a girl."

"You noticed, huh? The word is *lady*."

"Yeah, well, whatever. Turk'll make mincemeat out of her in the first twenty-four hours."

"They're sending Turk to the Island?" Even as he asked the question, he knew the answer. Turk Solitto had been a school-yard bully who grew into a fifteen-year-old cocky son of a bitch. He'd conned his probation officers with the finesse of a master, giving the Rhode Island rehab programs a massive shock. The Island was the state's final attempt to curb his delinquency.

Keely would get the opportunity to test her dream with a nightmare like Turk.

Oakes finished his beer, belched again and crushed the can in one hand. Lighting a cigar that smelled like burned broccoli, he said, "That's what I heard this morning. All the tape decks for miles around us are sighing with relief. Seems the court didn't know what else to do with him. Too bad about your lady.''

"She's not *my* lady." No, not his lady, but the Judge's daughter. Aw, hell.

"Then how come you look so worried? Come to think of it, I ain't seen you look that rattled since you heard the Judge croaked.''

Jed had found that in life there were certain things a lot of thinking didn't improve or change. Gut knowledge could be a real pain at times. Turk with Keely. The possibilities made his blood run cold. He didn't want to worry about Keely Lockwood. He didn't want to go to the Island when he knew it wouldn't survive the summer. But he sure didn't like the idea of Turk being the one to bring on the downfall.

He told himself this change in plans had a lot to do with obligation and gratitude to the Judge. It had nothing to do with Keely's spirit or her violet scent or her smile. It had to do with the Judge's daughter staying in one piece. Her turning into mincemeat would be sacrilege.

Chapter 2

In her beach house in Newport, an hour after she'd left Jed's apartment in Providence, Keely poured iced tea for herself and for her mother. She'd changed into light blue shorts and an old bikini top, and had dispensed with her sandals.

"I assume from the disappointed look on your face that things didn't go as you'd planned," Rosemary Lockwood said. She was arranging a bunch of daisies and wild iris that Keely had unceremoniously dumped into a water-filled mayonnaise jar.

Except for their honey-brown hair, mother and daughter contrasted with each other. Rosemary was tall and willowy to Keely's small size. Keely envied her mother's panache and style, and wondered now if panache and style would have convinced Jed. But then Rosemary would have walked over hot coals before she would have bribed her way into a strange man's apartment.

Keely handed her mother one of the glasses. "Oh, they went exactly as I planned. All except for the outcome."

Rosemary gave the flowers an appraising look. "Whatever happened to that lovely crystal vase the Morrows gave you?"

"Paul has it," Keely said with a shrug. "Vases belong in condos, Mom. Beach houses are strictly mayonnaise-jar style."

She'd bought the beach house after she divorced Paul, and deliberately gave it a casual look. Four rooms and a small bath that would send an interior decorator into early retirement, but Keely wanted to spend her time at home relaxing, not worrying about the decor.

The throw rugs were of colorful cotton, and the furniture was soft and accommodating. The major piece was an overstuffed bookcase. It was filled with sociology books, a variety of fiction from classics to horror, poetry books by some obscure poets who Keely decided had probably starved to death in garrets from lack of recognition.

Then there were the *Cooking for Two* cookbooks she'd collected during her four-year marriage. Emphasis on collect, Paul had commented more than once. So she wasn't a great cook, she'd told him with a breezy wave of her hand. That was why someone created takeout.

She led the way out to the deck, which was made private by sand dunes that bordered the beach beyond. The horizon was preparing itself for a glorious sunset. Keely sprawled on one of the poppy-red-cushioned lounges, while her mother chose a matching chair.

Rosemary brushed a wisp of hair off her cheek. "Tell me what happened."

"He refused to come to the Island."

Keely took a long sip of her tea and watched a sea gull swoop down after some morsel. Later she intended to run on the beach, work up a good hard sweat and get Jed Corey out of her mind.

"I gathered that. Did he give a reason?"

"A stupid one."

Her mother swirled her lemon slice through her tea, watching Keely and waiting. "Well?"

Keely told her about the visit, what Jed had said, and to her surprise, the only thing that made Rosemary lift her eyebrows was the quotation from the book of Ecclesiastes in the Bible.

"Forget it, Mom. Jed Corey isn't religious."

"Religion isn't just going to church on Sunday," Rosemary replied, crossing her slender legs. "It sounds like his religion is more practical than spiritual."

"I think I would have preferred the spiritual. Then he'd feel guilty and do as I ask."

"What a thing to say! Surely you don't want him to come out of guilt?"

Keely drew up her knees and sighed. "No, I suppose not. Dad looked for honesty and dedication."

"And practicality and stability. He felt the kids needed adults with as few problems as possible. Those poor kids have had enough traumas to fill a few textbooks." Rosemary took a delicate sip of tea, and Keely wondered if her father ever appreciated what a really dazzling person her mother was. "Guilt," Rosemary added, "would be a poor basis for a working relationship between Jed and the kids."

"Jed would have been great with them. There's a solidness—I don't know, maybe that's the wrong word." Keely thought for a moment. "Inner strength? Something. I know he would have been perfect."

Rosemary stood and walked over to the railing. Her daffodil-yellow skirt blew up slightly. "How did he look?"

The question startled Keely. The answer that popped into her mind had nothing to do with his coming or not coming to the Island. It had everything to do with his gray-and-silver eyes, and the chest hair she'd felt for about a half second.

Disturbing, she thought, sexually disturbing, but to her mother she said, "Controlled."

"Sexy?"

Keely blinked, then coughed at the gulp of tea that went down the wrong way. "Mom, really! Sexy? I barely noticed his looks."

Rosemary turned around. "Now I don't believe that. He's a very attractive man. You must have noticed."

Anxious to get off the subject, she turned the question back on her mother. "And how would you know?"

"Don't forget I knew a lot of the boys who went through the Black Horse program. Even after you and I moved off the Island, your father shared a lot of his concerns about the kids. Jed held a special place in Edgar's heart."

Keely felt the lingering loss at the mention of her father. It was one more reason why she wanted to work on the Island and make the program succeed as it had done when he was the director. Black Horse was special to him, and therefore it would be special to her. She wasn't looking for any state commendations or rewards, but only for Black Horse to again become what her father dreamed it could be.

"Keely?"

She glanced at her mother. "I'm going to have to call Seth and tell him I'll look into getting someone else."

"Have you considered what Jed said? He could be right."

Keely sighed. She knew her mother wasn't pleased with the idea of her daughter's spending her life with troubled boys.

"He's wrong. You know how Dad felt. He spent most of his time on that Island and you whiled away the years playing bridge and going to the garden club." Her mother paled slightly and Keely could have kicked herself for being so blunt.

Edgar Lockwood had taken the term *dedicated public servant* seriously. He'd wanted to do more than hand down decisions and jail sentences from the family court bench. When he heard Rhode Island wanted a director for a new program for troubled boys, he'd resigned and taken the position. Keely had been nine years old.

She and her mother lived on the Island for six months, but Rosemary had found the isolation too lonely. Keely knew that she, too, had been a consideration. The Island was no place for a teenage girl to live.

Her parents hadn't divorced. Her father had visited them in Newport often, but Keely knew his heart was with kids like Jed. On the one hand, she'd realized her father's work demanded time away from his family, and yet on the other she'd seen the loneliness in her mother's life, the desire to be a supportive partner, but also the need to be supported.

"A good part of the time was spent raising you," her mother said, graciously allowing the comment to pass. "Although to look at you, now that you're thirty, I wonder if I ever had any influence on you. Even four years in college and marriage to Paul didn't seem to affect you."

Keely flipped her braid over her shoulder. "You did a great job. One of these days I'll emerge like a butterfly."

Rosemary's look was dubious. "I won't hold my breath. You are what you are—a little offbeat and too determined, but then so was your father. I never saw him happier than when he was talking about the Island and the boys." A wistfulness filled her eyes, and Keely thought she saw a sheen of tears.

Rosemary sat down in the chair again, suddenly appearing tired. "I can't believe eight months have passed. It seems like only weeks." Edgar Lockwood's death had come in his sleep on the weekend before Christmas. Heart failure, the doctor had said.

How sad, Keely thought, to love a man who found his happiness somewhere other than in the woman he married. She allowed the silence of the summer afternoon to stretch between them, not sure if she could trust her voice.

They didn't speak for a few minutes, each reminded of the sense of loss they'd felt since his death. Finally, Keely changed the subject. "Maybe Seth will have some ideas."

"You can't go by yourself, you know." Rosemary allowed the words to slide out carefully, but Keely didn't miss the hopeful sound.

"We've been through this, Mom. It's something I want to do. No, more than that, it's something I have to do."

Rosemary looked out toward the sand dunes. Beach grass swayed in the breeze. A few hundred yards away came the shouts of children playing on the beach.

"He came to the funeral, you know," Rosemary said, turning around.

"Seth? Yes, I know."

"Not Seth. Jed Corey."

Keely sat up, her legs straddling the lounge chair. "Jed Corey? I didn't see him."

Rosemary put her glass down on a small table. "He kept in the distance. I saw him standing near the cemetery entrance. I had the strangest feeling when I looked up and noticed him there. It was as if he wanted to be included, but he was afraid to come any closer."

The December day had been raw and cold, Keely recalled. When they'd all hurried to the cars to leave, her mother had excused herself for a moment. Keely had assumed she wanted to say one last goodbye at the grave.

"You talked to Jed, didn't you?" She tried to conjure up an image of her mother and Jed Corey together and failed.

"Yes. I wanted him to come back to the house, but he wouldn't."

"Of course he wouldn't," she said too quickly, wondering where the sureness of her answer had come from. It had nothing to do with class distinctions, but with the man Jed was. Her mother's answer clarified it for her.

"He asked me if it was all right if he came to see me another time. He wanted to pay his respects and share some things your father had told him."

"Why didn't you ever tell me about that?" He could have paid his respects by agreeing to come to the Island, she thought, not in the least bit guilty about her feelings. He certainly had no compunction about expressing his.

"I'm not sure. I guess because Jed seemed like such a private person."

"Did he come and see you?"

She smiled. "Yes. It was a warm day for January, and he'd ridden a motorcycle. He wore a leather jacket, and I believe the rest of his clothes were black. It was a commanding sight."

Keely thought of her mother's pristine house with its white carpets and French Provincial furniture. An unexpected picture of Jed standing amid all that delicacy sent an erotic shiver down her back. There it was again, she thought, liking the sensation and at the same time telling herself that she was indulging in some far-fetched fantasy.

"What did he say? About Dad, I mean."

"He talked about some of the kids who failed in the program, and your father's feelings of inadequacy in not getting through to them. Things of that nature."

Keely didn't miss her mother's refusal to meet her eyes. "That's all?"

"Yes." She finished her tea, fascinated suddenly by a sparrow teetering on a bush. "I thought we were going to have dinner," she said, her gaze coming back to Keely. "I brought lobster salad and rolls. I'll set the table while you make coffee." She brushed her hands together in a gesture of dismissal and went into the house.

In the kitchen, Keely put the glasses in the dishwasher. "Mom? Come on, you can't just drop it there."

Rosemary tucked a tea towel around her waist. "Yes, I can." She lifted the bowl of lobster salad out of the refrigerator and put it on the counter.

Keely frowned, puzzled by the abrupt answer. What did it matter? she thought. Jed wasn't coming to the Island. She'd probably never see him again.

Her mother sighed. "All right. I'm respecting Jed's privacy. Some of the things he shared about your father were very personal. I don't think it's my place to repeat them."

Keely digested that. She respected privacy, too, although today she hadn't acted as if she did. Bribing her way into his apartment, looking through his scrapbook and then assuming he was going to drop whatever life he had and follow her to the Island didn't show her in a very professional light.

A wave of shame washed over her. Her father would not have been pleased by her methods.

Dinner was somewhat strained with both women keeping the topics on neutral ground. After they'd had coffee and cleaned the dishes, Keely's mother gathered her into her arms for a long hug.

"Darling, I don't want you to bury your life on the Island."

"I might not be going, if I don't find someone to replace Jed."

"Do you want me to go and see him?"

Keely knew her mother would rather die than venture alone into a man's apartment. "You'd do that for me, wouldn't you?" she asked, honestly amazed.

"I don't know what I could say to convince him, but I could try."

"You're sweet to offer, but it wouldn't do any good. He left no possibilities open that he might change his mind."

Later, on the telephone with Seth, Keely explained that Jed would not be coming.

She could hear the worry in his voice. "What are you gonna do?"

"Try to find someone else. What about that guy with the beard who worked there last summer? Dad told me he volunteered after hearing about the program on a radio talk show."

"No, forget about him. Last I heard he was in California. Went back to get his degree at some college."

"Damn," she muttered, disgusted with the predicament she was in, and angry at Jed for putting her in it.

Again, Seth expressed his concern about not having Jed at the Island. Keely sighed and looked at the stack of manila folders on her desk, each more than an inch thick. They contained the histories of the kids she'd be greeting in two days. Kids who, even though she didn't like to admit it, would have benefited from Jed.

"Let me do some thinking tonight. When I come tomorrow, we'll talk. We have to get someone or I'll be in trouble with the board. I plan to be on the 7:00 a.m. ferry. Is the staff already there? Has the coast guard been notified that the Island is functioning again? Has Irma got the kitchen all stocked?"

"Yep to all three. And Irma, she can't wait to start cooking."

At least Keely didn't have to worry about feeding the kids. Nearing sixty, Irma Wilson had cooked for the Island for the past ten years. Keely knew that part of the reason she stayed was Seth. They were both alone and had grown close over the years. Keely couldn't have been more pleased.

She hung up the phone and sat down to read through the folders she'd picked up at the courthouse before going to see Jed.

She adjusted her glasses and began with Dennis "Turk" Solitto. Fifteen. Father deceased. Mother worked in a jewelry manufacturing plant. Oldest of three children. Aggressive manner with a tendency to lose his temper when confronted by authority. Didn't they all? she thought as she turned the page.

Exceptionally bright and worked well with his hands. Arrested five times. She read the list of things he'd been arrested for: car theft, shoplifting, drinking, vandalism—the list went on. She made a mental note of the "exceptionally bright." Sad, she thought. As in many cases she'd dealt with in Family Services, the problem with very intelligent kids lay in channeling their energy into something constructive.

She read through the courtroom notes and finally came to a letter that Turk's mother had written. The paper was cheap five-and-dime stationery, but there was nothing shoddy about the emotion behind the words.

Please give Dennis another chance, the mother pleaded. *He ain't bad, he tries to do right, it's just so hard when everything goes wrong. I try to watch him, to make him be good. I don't know why I failed. I'll try harder. I need him at home. Please give him another chance....*

Keely brushed the tears from her eyes at the desperation and frustration in the note. She wished there was some magic solution that would take away all the poverty and problems. Mrs. Solitto was going through a bitter, heartbreaking experience, but to her credit, she hadn't abandoned her son.

When Turk left the Island, Keely knew, he'd need his mother's support to keep his life going in the right direction.

Direction that rested on her shoulders, Keely realized solemnly.

For the next hour she read through the rest of the files, finding similarities and more sadness. She closed the last one, laid her glasses on top of the pile and stood to stretch.

It was nine-thirty. Knowing she still had to finish packing, she nevertheless wandered out onto the deck. The ocean made a thunderous sound that wasn't as noticeable during the day. She listened, stepped off the deck and walked toward the shore.

She picked up her pace, running lightly across the dunes and down onto the flat sand. Setting an even rhythm, she started down the beach. The warm wind, smelling of suntan lotion, blew across her face.

Jed lingered in her mind, so she ran harder. Concentrating on her breathing, she tried to focus her thoughts to tomorrow and whom she could get to take his place.

As she passed a lifeguard stand, she realized she'd had Jed on her mind almost constantly since she'd left his apartment. Men were not a constant in her life or her mind.

Her marriage to Paul Morrow had failed not because of lack of communication, but because Paul had wanted and expected too much from her. He had wanted someone who would pick up after him and prepare meals that didn't come from the microwave, and who would turn into a sex goddess in the bedroom.

The bedroom she could handle; it was the dirty socks and piecrust that had turned her off. She simply couldn't do it all nor had she thought she had to. Paul didn't agree. Finally the one place where they'd found some compatibility—the bedroom—went the way of the dirty socks and the homemade piecrust.

Keely moved closer to the water, running along the edge; the sand was clumpy and cold beneath her feet.

Now if she were sexually repressed and was looking for some man to turn her on, the funny flutters she felt when she thought about Jed would make sense. But she was none of those things. In fact, she was happy with an uncomplicated life. She liked her freedom and her privacy. Perhaps it was just as well that Jed wasn't coming to the Island. She'd have her hands full with the kids. She didn't need any complications.

Forty-five minutes later, she slowed her pace to a walk, cooling down, letting her body settle. She came to a stop, and as she did whenever she ran at night, she took off her top and slipped out of her shorts. She ran into the water and swam quickly, enjoying the coolness against her skin.

Her body felt free and one with the elements. She turned on her back and floated. The black sky dressed in silver stars spread above her with a timeless majesty. She'd miss this on the Island. There was a beautiful beach, but skinny-dipping would be out of the question.

Her unfinished packing awaited her, and reluctantly she allowed her feet to touch bottom. She walked out of the water. The moonlight shimmered across the sand as she picked up her clothes.

Naked, she climbed the dunes, her shorts and top dangling in one hand. Before she got to the deck, she saw him.

Dressed in jeans and a black T-shirt, he sat on the farthest end of the deck's railing. His back rested against a corner support beam of the house, and his legs stretched out along the top of the rail. His ankles were crossed and his black boots were worn and scuffed. In one hand, he held a can of soda. His black leather jacket lay on her lounge, and she wondered if his motorcycle was parked beside her car.

He toasted her with the soda. "You're out of beer."

She didn't move, holding her clothes close to her body and telling herself she wasn't really standing there naked in front of Jed Corey. Any minute she'd awaken.

"I hate beer," she said automatically.

He came off the railing slowly and with such smoothness that Keely thought he'd floated. Her body began to shake and she didn't trust her voice.

Jed crossed the deck, putting the can on the table where Keely and her mother had eaten dinner. He stared out into the black night. His hair caught a sprinkling of moonbeams, and Keely had the strangest thought that if she swept her hand through the soft blackness, she'd capture a handful of light.

"Nice place you have here," he said in a low distant voice. "Private and quiet."

Didn't he know she was naked? Don't be stupid, she told herself. She expected some raunchy remark or at the very least a look that showed he noticed. Here she was naked and shivering, and he'd glanced at her as if she were one of the sand dunes. He continued to look off into the distance, leaning slightly forward. His hands gripped the rail, his hips shifting slightly to one side.

He's giving me a chance to get into the house, she realized suddenly, stunned by the gesture. No words, no apologies for being there or catching her at an awkward moment. Just an ordinary turn of his head.

"Excuse me," she murmured, and hurried into the house. As she passed him, she thought she heard him exhale with a shudder.

In her bedroom, she leaned against the door, her own breath fighting for space in her lungs. She dropped her clothes on the floor, hugged her arms around herself and counted to twenty.

Finally, when she could hear something other than the pounding of her heart, she heard the screen door leading to the deck close. She listened for footsteps and heard none. Was he staying outside? Had he left? A rush of disappointment went through her. Then she heard her desk chair hit the squeaky floorboards in the living room.

Relieved that he'd stayed, and not wanting to think about why, she made her way into the bathroom. She took a hot shower and shampooed her hair. As she was blowing it dry a few minutes later, she found herself impatient to see him. Why was he here? Had he changed his mind?

She suddenly stopped the sweeping motion of the dryer. Had her mother called him? A surge of anger shot through her at his ready compliance to her mother's request.

"Ouch!" she yelped when the hair dryer overheated one spot on her scalp. She rubbed the place, then quickly finished.

Most of her clothes were packed, so she opted for a pair of sweatpants and an old college sweatshirt. She brushed her hair, its length reaching six inches down her back. She tucked her hair up with barrettes, exposing her ears. She decided her cheeks were too pink, and her green eyes as bright and eager as a teenager's on her first date.

Disgusted with the path her thoughts were taking, she grimaced at her reflection. Now why should he notice anything as ordinary as the brightness in her eyes? He hadn't raised an eyebrow at her nudity.

She opened the bedroom door, her pulse rate picking up, but when she saw him she couldn't stop a small laugh.

He lay stretched out on her couch, one of the manila folders in his hands. Perched on his nose were her glasses. They made him seem vulnerable and accessible, and Keely felt relieved of any necessity to explain her nudity to him. Not that he deserved an explanation, or that one was even warranted.

Still, she didn't want him to think she was an exhibitionist, and she had to admit their first meeting hadn't exactly shown her in the best light.

He looked up. He didn't remove the glasses, but he did lower the folder. The lamp on her desk cast its light across his long, lean body. His shirt was faded to a many-times-washed gray; the short sleeves hugged the muscles in his arms.

She stepped into the living room. "I see you've made yourself comfortable," she said. "Can you see out of those?"

"They're not very strong. I was curious as to why you don't wear contacts."

"They irritate my eyes. The glasses are mostly for reading." She straightened some of the folders on her desk.

Keeping the glasses on, he made no effort to sit up or move from the couch. "Swimming alone at night is dangerous, Keely."

No mention of her nudity. "I've done it since I moved here two years ago. I don't go out far, not even over my head." She picked up the can of soda he'd opened, found it almost full and took a long sip, remembering how he'd drunk from her glass that afternoon. "But you're not here to talk about my swimming."

"I do want to talk about you doing dangerous things."

"Like what?"

"Like taking the directorship at the Island."

"I've already taken it," she said, putting down the can on the coffee table. "Besides, I would hardly put that in the dangerous classification."

"Have you read these files? Particularly the one on Solitto?" She noted the slight edge in his tone as though what he really wanted to say might shock her.

"Jed, I appreciate your concern, but I'm a big girl. I've worked with teenagers since I graduated from college. I know the potential problems."

"Name some."

"What?"

"Name some potential problems."

"Drugs. Drinking. Guns or weapons of some type. None of those are allowed on the Island, so they don't even come under the heading of potential problems."

"Smuggling some kind of weapon onto the Island is not impossible," he said, giving her a long intense look. "But you left out something. The kids. They're the potential problems. Drugs, booze and the weapon of choice are only the beginning. Remove them and the kids will find others. In this case, you, Keely. Teenage boys love to prove their masculinity. As director, you'll be a challenge they'll welcome."

She wanted to tell him that if he was really concerned, he'd come with her, but then she remembered her unprofessional feelings toward him, and decided it was better that he wasn't concerned.

"I don't need a lecture on teenage behavior or misbehavior. If you came here to warn me, then I appreciate it, but I can take care of myself."

Slowly he removed the glasses, placed them on the table and laid the file beside them. "Come over here."

The three tiny words drifted to her and through her and wound around her like silken ribbons of heat. "I don't want to."

"Are you afraid of me?"

"Should I be?"

He looked at her for a long moment. Then he extended his hand, palm up, fingers relaxed. "I think we can handle it."

Handle what? she questioned silently. But she didn't have to ask; she knew. And to her annoyance she wasn't sure if she wanted to handle it. But then she told herself that was nonsense. The tremor of attraction she felt for him wasn't some signal to dive into a . . . what? Relationship? The word didn't fit with Jed. To dive into the nearest bed? In this case hers? No. She had no intention of doing that, either. She'd never indulged in instant-attraction sex. Never. She cursed the tightening of her breasts and the weakness in her legs.

Determined to prove she could handle it—whatever "it" might entail—she took the few steps needed to stand beside him, and slowly placed her hand in his.

He didn't tighten his fingers or pull her down next to him. His palm was callused and bumpy against her softer one, and she felt his strength and control. She doubted that he ever hit a nail wrong, or that when he held a woman he would have to use force.

When she lifted her lashes and looked at him, his eyes seemed more mysterious.

"I'm not your type," he reminded her.

Keely closed her eyes. "Jed, this is really silly."

"I think the word is chemistry. It happens sometimes."

"Well, it can't happen this time."

" 'To every thing there is a season,' " he murmured so softly that she wondered if it was a promise he intended to keep someday.

Finally he tightened his fingers around hers and gently urged her to sit down. He shifted over to give her room. She perched on the edge of the couch, feeling stupid, embarrassed and immature.

"About the Island," she began, wanting to let the whole subject of chemistry and seasons die a silent death. "I talked to Seth, and I'm sure we can get someone else. I appreciate your concern, although I told Mother not to go and see you."

"She didn't come to see me."

"Then why are you here?"

"To try and persuade you not to take the directorship. I told you that a few minutes ago. Since you're determined to go, you leave me no choice."

"Choice about what?"

"I'm going to the Island with you."

Chapter 3

He'd changed his mind.

It was what she wanted, wasn't it? Wasn't that the reason she'd gone to see him? Hadn't she told her mother he'd be perfect? The Children in Crisis board would be happy, and there would be no need for a frantic hunt for a replacement.

She pulled her hand away and stood.

He made no move to stop her. "Not what you were expecting to hear, is it?"

"I wanted to hear it this afternoon. Now I have the distinct feeling you're coming as some sort of guardian of my life."

He placed his hands behind his head, settled himself even more comfortably into the couch and made no denials.

"Dammit, Jed! That's what you're doing, isn't it?"

"Yes."

"What if I'd never come to see you? What if I'd gotten someone else?"

"It wouldn't have mattered." Didn't he ever raise his voice?

"You'd have come anyway."

"Yes."

"Why?"

"I don't want anything to happen to the Judge's daughter."

This has gone far enough, she thought. "How did I manage to live for thirty years without your protection?" she asked sarcastically.

"It isn't the past thirty that concern me, it's the next thirty."

A mixture of feelings stirred through her—security because he was worried about her, and indignation because he thought she needed him. "Is this some code of the street?"

"My code."

Of course. Hadn't Seth told her Jed lived by his own rules? "This is crazy, Jed. We're not living in the nineteenth century."

He studied her, making her feel naive. "No, but it's a lot more dangerous. Don't turn this into a battle between the two of us. We can get along okay if—"

"If I do as I'm told?" she interrupted, planting her hands on her hips. "If I behave? If I let Jed Corey take care of me?"

"*If*, Keely." He came off the couch in a slow, smooth motion. "If you worry about the kids' hearts and getting them on the right track. That's what your father did." He reached behind her, not touching her, and lifted his leather jacket off the back of her chair.

What could she say to that? She could hardly argue, but still she thought his reason was archaic. This was the nineties. She hardly needed a protector; nothing dark and sinister was about to sweep her away and make sure she was never seen again.

He shrugged into his jacket, those gray eyes appearing to see deeply into her thoughts. That made her think he was the dark and sinister something plotting to sweep her away.

One thing she'd learned quickly about him: he didn't chatter or offer long-winded explanations of what he'd said. There were no "in other words" sentences. His statements were like well-thought-out decrees, giving little room for argument.

At her back door he said, "Good night," zipped up his jacket and strode out to a motorcycle so black that it was almost invisible.

Keely watched him straddle the bike. It roared to life with an ear-shattering growl in the quiet summer night. Sand and gravel spit and scurried out from under the tires as he took off up the road. Keely slammed the door, the clunk nowhere near as loud as Jed's exit. Her heart throbbed with an anticipation she neither sought nor wanted.

She turned out the lights and locked up. In her bedroom, she finished packing. By the time she'd pulled on a blue cotton nightie with a rainbow on the front, and vigorously brushed her teeth, she knew that if she allowed herself, she'd be in deep trouble when it came to Jed Corey.

Why couldn't he simply be the male presence in the Island? Why couldn't he be benign and unremarkable like Paul? Why did he keep a scrapbook? Why did he have eyes that, when he looked at her, made her knees feel squishy and at the same time raised a thirst in her soul? Why did he feel a primitive need to protect her?

"And why didn't he even blink when I was naked?"

She tossed her cosmetics into a small zippered case and shoved it into the corner of her duffel bag.

In the living room, she picked up her glasses where he'd tossed them. A smile touched her mouth as she remembered the whimsical sight of the very cool and controlled Jed Corey wearing her glasses.

There seemed to be no end to his ability to surprise her. His absolutely unaffected reaction to her nudity had so stunned her that the obvious embarrassment she should have felt when she faced him dressed had never materialized.

She put the glasses into their case. Before tucking them into her handbag, she peered at its contents, then dumped them all on her desk. The rubber-banded roll of bills that Jed had tossed in fell out. Her father had wrapped money that he kept at home the same way. Interesting, she thought, as well as revealing. Wasn't imitation the greatest form of flattery? Flattery, however, seemed too shallow for Jed.

She put the money back in her handbag, deciding she'd thought about him enough for one day. She sorted through the rest of the contents and threw into a nearby wastebasket old recipes, crumpled tissues, a cracked pen and the broken nail file she'd used to pick her car lock the day she left her keys dangling in the ignition. She found a lipstick she'd been hunting for, as well as two unpaid parking tickets.

No one paid parking tickets, she told herself as she added them to the trash. One she had gotten when she had a meeting with the Children in Crisis board and couldn't find a parking place. She'd double-parked.

Rhode Islanders double-parked all the time, which was what she told the meter maid, who eyed her as if she'd robbed a bank and then said, ''The Judge would be shocked, Ms. Lockwood.''

Shock might have been a little too strong a word, but her father had certainly been a stickler about obeying the law.

The tickets lay on top of the crumpled tissues, and when her annoyed stare didn't cause them to disintegrate, she plucked them out, signed the waivers on the back, wrote a check and stuffed them into an envelope.

She crunched a mouthful of candy and rolled the switchblade around in her hand in a poor imitation of Jed's expertise that afternoon. The knife wasn't hers. She'd taken it from a twelve-year-old boy named Sean, who could have been a double for Tom Sawyer, except for the street-savvy blue eyes and the lethal threat to ''gut'' her secretary.

Keely had come out of her office in time to hear a list of four-letter words. Debbie, white and trembling, looked as if she might die of fright before the knife ever touched her. Without thinking that this kid could easily gut her as well, Keely demanded he put the knife on the desk. When he refused, using a few more colorful words, Keely replied with a few of her own.

Later, when her good sense caught up with her actions, she realized it was her lavender dress with lace on the bodice and sleeves, pearl stud earrings and hair arranged in a style more feminine than she usually wore for work that had given her the edge. It wasn't her rather questionable ability of disarming kids with knives sharper than she had at home in her kitchen drawer. Sean had simply wilted into a chair, embarrassed when he realized he'd been taken out by a woman.

Keely understood his shattered pride, as she did the tough image that kids like Sean needed to exist. However, endangering her secretary was a whole other question. When Debbie's color finally returned and her breathing resumed, Keely assured her that knife threats weren't a daily occurrence.

She debated now whether she should put the knife back in her handbag or leave it in her desk. She'd carried it now for two weeks without any problems, and besides, it had helped to reinforce her image with Jed.

And exactly what kind of image did she want to reinforce? That she was capable? Tough? Or did she want the image of a daughter so loved by her father that he would want her to continue his work?

Keely put the knife in her handbag, the last question troubling her. Of course she believed her father loved her. She closed the flap, fiddling with the fringe while she concentrated on projecting a capable and tough image.

She straightened her desk and pushed everything she didn't know what to do with into the top drawer. Once again she went through Turk's folder, recalling Jed's warning.

What if she'd said, "All right, I won't take the directorship"? Jed was obviously better acquainted with kids like Turk than she, but she wasn't exactly a fragile flower who'd just stepped out of do-gooders' school with plans to clean up the streets using love and understanding.

She'd seen the filthy tenements. She'd held mothers whose fourteen-year-old children shouldn't have experienced anything more serious than a broken arm, yet were lifeless from drug overdose. She'd wept with them over deaths that should have been sixty years into the future.

Turk was dangerous, and so were the others who would come to the Island. But this was their last chance. That was why they were going there. That was why she was going there.

"I'm going to the Island with you," Jed had said. Though she shrank from the idea that she needed protection, she acknowledged Jed's presence would be a deterrent. And that was where it ended. He would be there to assist her. Period. Not to run roughshod over the kids, not to protect her, but to help her make the Island a success once again.

At 3:00 a.m., her eyes had counted every paint-roller sweep on her bedroom ceiling. The ocean roared up onto the beach signaling high tide, but the sound she heard was the growl of Jed's motorcycle, the clamor of her unsteady heart when he'd said, "Come over here" and the thunderous approach of the coming weeks.

Working with him, being with him . . .

She raised herself on her elbows and glared out the screened window at the starry sky. "This is insanity. He's not my type. He likes it that way and so do I."

She punched her pillow, flopped on her back and made a herculean effort to concentrate on what her life had been like before this afternoon. How could one man whom—if she counted the exact moments—she'd been with a total of one hour, twelve minutes and fourteen seconds, have managed to jumble her thoughts and keep her awake? Yet here he was embedded in her mind. . . .

The moon wheeled out from behind a cloud, and for a few silent moments, Black Horse Island disappeared from her thoughts.

"No," she whispered, dragging the sheet up to her chin, clutching for the elusive ripples of her father's dream. She turned her back on the moon—and tried to close her heart to Jed Corey.

The sun was making its eastern climb when Keely parked her car in the small rutted parking lot in front of Aquidneck Dock.

She'd overslept and was annoyed with herself as a result. She'd dressed quickly in a loose-fitting turquoise jumpsuit, cuffed at the ankles, and white tennis shoes with no socks. In ten minutes she'd packed the car, then grabbed her handbag and her hairbrush from the house before locking the door. Now, trying to see more of herself in the visor mirror than just the dark circles under her eyes, she braided her hair.

"Good morning."

Keely jumped, swinging around to face Jed Corey. He'd obviously had no trouble sleeping. He studied her with a curiosity that, if she had been less agitated and tired, would have made her smile and say something clever. Instead, she plaited her hair wrong and had to comb it out and start again.

"Morning," she mumbled as she tried to concentrate on what her fingers were doing. At the same time she noticed that his hair was still damp, that he smelled too good, too male, that the sleeves of his black sweatshirt were pushed up over his elbows, that his arms were tanned and muscled and that even the veins in his wrist were tight. His jeans, however, weren't snug, but they fit him with a sexy comfort that seemed to say he didn't need to flaunt his masculinity.

She let out a long breath, and again had to undo her braid and begin once more.

He braced one arm on the car roof and squinted toward the ferry dock. "I thought maybe you decided to take my advice."

She paused, her fingers on the braid. She knew he meant changing her mind about the directorship. "You're under no obligation to come with me, Mr. Corey. Strong males are not exactly extinct in Rhode Island. I can easily find someone else."

He didn't say anything but followed the slow movement of a small fishing boat chugging up the bay. Finally, he looked at her. "I believe we settled that last night, Ms. Lockwood."

She met his gaze as she finished the braid, twisting a rubber band around the end. "I might still change my mind, you know."

He took his hand off the roof and opened the door. "You won't. You're too stubborn and gutsy. Come on, you need to get your stuff down to the dock."

She frowned as she put her brush away and took the keys from the ignition. A compliment, of sorts. Or had he just wanted to end the conversation?

"Keely, does the duffel bag go, too?"

Jed held her suitcase and briefcase in one hand and was reaching for the stuffed duffel.

"Yes, it goes, too. Here, let me take the briefcase."

He allowed her that, and they walked side by side down to the loading dock. Also waiting to go on the ferry were a pile of new single mattresses wrapped in plastic, a box of textbooks, new baseball equipment, two cartons of fresh fruit and Jed's two duffels. One looked like an Army issue and the other carried a St. Mark's logo. Beside them sat his toolbox. Keely wondered if he'd brought his scrapbook.

"You didn't bring all this on the motorcycle, did you?" she asked, setting the briefcase down beside his toolbox.

"Yeah. A friend wanted to use my truck. Since I won't be needing it for a few weeks, I let him have it. The bike will carry a lot if you pack tight." He put her stuff down beside his, and it suddenly struck her that with their belongings all nestled together they could easily be mistaken for a couple.

She didn't see his motorcycle, and she was about to ask him where he'd parked it when he said, "Is someone going to pick up your car?"

"Yes, my neighbor. Later this afternoon."

He nodded. "Good."

"What about your motorcycle?"

He pointed to a sagging garage with lobster pots piled up along one side. He told her his bike was inside.

Jed peeled a five-dollar bill out of his jeans pocket and handed it to a boy wearing denim cutoffs. About eight years old, he had scruffy black hair and a smile that promised to break female hearts in a few years. He was coiling what looked to Keely like enough rope to reach from Rhode Island to California.

"Willy, watch this stuff, okay?"

"Sure, Jed." Willy pocketed the money and moved his rope-coiling task closer to their belongings. "Ma's workin' in the diner. You gonna see her?"

Jed ruffled Willy's hair. "That's why I came early." He glanced at Keely. "How about some breakfast? The ferry won't leave for another hour."

Breakfast sounded heavenly. She told herself that her immediate curiosity about Willy's mother was just that.

The Ferry Slip Diner did most of its business between two and five in the morning when the fishing boats were going out. By seven the customers were mostly locals, and a few tourists who were either lost or had found out the diner served a mammoth breakfast for $2.50.

Jed touched the small of Keely's back as they stepped inside.

Bacon, the garlicky smell of chourico—a hot Portuguese sausage and a staple of the Rhode Island cuisine, Portuguese or not—strong coffee and music on the jukebox, welcomed them.

"The Ferry Slip is a historic structure," Jed said to Keely in a not too serious tone. "The owners cleaned off the grime and grease and put on a new door."

Keely laughed.

"There's a booth," he murmured so close to her ear that she felt his warm breath. He kept his hand on her back and guided her down the narrow space past age-nicked tables, lumpy seats and comments by the locals.

At the empty booth, Jed slid into one side and she slid into the other. On the red table were paper place mats with the menu printed on them, silverware that looked like its every trip through the diner's dishwasher was an endurance test and a sticky sugar holder.

A waitress headed toward them. She was red-haired and busty, with a face that could have been beautiful but instead was simply pretty. Her smile was warm, friendly—and all for Jed.

"Jed!"

Keely knew this was Willy's mother.

Jed slid out of the booth with only enough time to straighten when the waitress sailed into his arms, giving him a kiss that was heady enough to bring a chuckle from a guy who straddled a counter stool.

Jed gave her another hug before releasing her. "Patsy, you look terrific."

"Thanks to you. The house is a dream, Jed. And Willy loves the yard and the swing you put up for him."

"I'm glad," he said simply.

She gave him a peck on the cheek, then leaned around to peer at Keely. "She's adorable, Jed. And braids."

Keely expected the next comment to be a request to see her report card.

"One braid, Patsy. And I like it."

Keely knew her eyes widened at this revelation. It seemed to say there was a vast difference between braids and *one braid*, which would have been astounding enough, but his adding that he liked it brought up deeper meanings that had nothing to do with hairstyle opinions.

Patsy stepped around Jed. "How do you do that? The French braiding, I mean. Do you have it done? This hair of mine is like tangled frizz. Thank God, Willy got his father's hair."

Keely's mind registered Willy's black hair and her eyes went to Jed's hair. Willy had called him Jed, hadn't he? To Patsy, she said, "I did it myself, but it took a lot of crooked tries before I got it right. By the way," she added, extending her hand to Patsy, "I'm Keely Lockwood. I met Willy outside."

Patsy shook her hand. "I'm Patsy Mendonca." She paused. "You ain't Judge Lockwood's daughter, are you?" At Keely's nod, she straightened and tapped three fingers against her cheek. "Well, if this ain't a coincidence. My girlfriend and me, we were talkin' about the Judge the other night. A real shame the way the Island has gone down the sewer since he died. Bet he's turnin' over in his grave with the grief of it. Oh—" Her cheeks turned even redder than the blusher had made them. "Oh, Ms. Lockwood, I'm sorry."

Keely's ears were ringing, and her words had a husky rawness to them. "It's okay. You're right. Dad would be very upset with what has happened at Black Horse."

Jed slipped into the booth beside Keely. He covered her chilled fingers with his warm ones and squeezed lightly.

"Patsy, give us a few minutes to look over the menu, and could you bring us some coffee?"

"Sure." She glided away, not in the least put out by Jed's subtle dismissal.

"Keely? You okay? Patsy means well, she just says whatever pops into her mind."

"She's right. The Island has gone down the sewer. And," she added, "Dad would be horrified."

Jed neither agreed nor disagreed. He let go of her hand but didn't slide out of the booth.

Keely rummaged beneath the switchblade in her handbag and pulled out her glasses. "Patsy seems to think you're pretty terrific." She put them on, and they promptly slid down her nose.

"Patsy's the one who's terrific," he said, settling back as though he never intended to move. "She's done a great job getting her life back on track. Cliff, her husband, went through the Island program a year after I left. Unfortunately, your father couldn't get through to him. A month after he left Black Horse he was back dealing drugs. After a bunch of arrests, he was finally convicted. He's in prison."

"Is he Willy's father?"

"No."

"Oh."

"And I'm not, either."

"That never occurred to me." Keely hoped her glasses hid her eyes enough so he wouldn't detect the lie.

"Yes, it did. Just like you're wondering if I sleep with Patsy."

"Do you?" It was a knee-jerk reaction, she told herself. "Jed, I'm sorry. That's none of my business." She studied the menu. "I think I'll have waffles."

Patsy returned with mugs of steaming coffee, took their order and left. Once again they were alone.

Keely felt as if she were in a cage, with the wall on one side, the table in front of her and Jed next to her. He turned his mug, added sugar, stirred and sampled.

She had no trouble envisioning Jed and Patsy together. She understood the appeal of a woman like Patsy. She was warm, open, maternal and probably offered more to a man than sexual release. And she certainly liked Jed. Thanks to you, she'd said when he told her she looked terrific. What had he done to generate that almost worshiping look besides put up a swing for Willy? Instinctively, Keely knew that whatever Patsy and Jed had together, it involved more than sex.

"I've never had sex with Patsy," he growled in a low tone.

Had he read her mind? She glanced at him, to find him looking at her with what seemed like an angry resentment.

"I don't like having to explain myself."

"I told you it was none of my business."

"Damn right it isn't, but for some insane reason, I don't want you to think I have."

Keely embraced the honesty of his words and his feelings. She slipped her fingers over his wrist. His pulse was jumping wildly. He pulled his hand away, straightened and slid out of the booth.

Keely grinned up at him.

"It isn't funny," he snapped.

"I wasn't laughing at you, Jed. I was just enjoying you opening up to me. You have this sort of controlled attitude that I find quite amazing." She almost said, *like when I was naked last night,* but decided it was better to let that die.

He swore again. This time the four-letter words made *damn* sound like kid stuff.

"Controlled emotions don't get you into trouble," he muttered. He seemed to be trying to decide whether to sit back down or go outside to clear his head.

"Here comes our breakfast," Keely said.

Patsy smiled and tried to shoo Jed back in beside Keely, but he sidestepped her and sat on the other side, mumbling about giving them each more room to eat.

The waffles Patsy placed in front of Keely were golden brown and surrounded by small link sausages. Jed had ordered chourico and scrambled eggs. Patsy refilled their mugs, placed butter and syrup in front of Keely and added three slices of buttered toast for Jed.

"Patsy, this looks wonderful," Keely said, suddenly starved and feeling lighthearted.

"Yeah, Patsy. It looks great."

She patted Jed's cheek. "You're too thin, you know."

Jed drew away from her hand with a grimace.

She grinned at Keely. "Nice meetin' you, Ms. Lockwood," she said shyly.

"Call me Keely, Patsy. I hope to see you again."

"Jed," Patsy said sternly. "You better not let this one get away. You messed things up with Marcie and she walked. Looks as if fate has given you another chance."

Jed gave Patsy a measured look. "Don't you have other customers you can hassle?"

Patsy stuck her tongue out at him. He glared at her with enough fury to set her hair on fire.

Keely watched the play by play as though it were a tennis match. On Keely's third mouthful of waffles, Patsy moved on to another table. Jed took a deep breath, eyed Keely with a don't-you-say-one-word look and then began to eat.

For the first time since she'd met Jed Corey, she felt as if she'd won a victory. Of sorts. Or maybe it was a small skirmish. But who was Marcie?

Marcie.

Jed hadn't given a lot of thought to Marcie since she married that bartender in Warwick.

He sat in the wheelhouse of the ferry, one foot resting on the other knee, and sipped muddy coffee that tasted like boiled socks, even with sugar added. Keely was on the deck, which was why he wasn't. The ferry was ten minutes out into the bay and chugging toward Black Horse Island.

He didn't particularly like Patsy's comment that he'd messed things up and Marcie walked, and he liked even less the startled look on Keely's face. It was bad enough admitting he didn't sleep with Patsy, but he'd be damned if he'd explain Marcie to Keely.

Sure he'd lived with Marcie. Sure their relationship had worked—for a while. But he'd never promised her anything like marriage or commitment, and he'd made sure Marcie understood that from the first day she moved in.

Mistakes, or messing things up as Patsy called it, were not something he made when it came to women. He never lied to them. Neither had he ever sputtered words about love and all that forever-after poetry that worked on Valentine's Day cards but rarely in reality.

And he didn't explain himself, either, but he had to Keely.

He let his foot drop to the floor, not wanting to think about why he was huddled in the wheelhouse, and why his thoughts seemed to be locked on one long brown braid and spring-green eyes that promised renewal and her eagerness to prove her abilities on the Island.

She'd commented at the diner about his control. The night before, he'd taken the ultimate control test when she walked up the sandy path silhouetted by the moon-light.

At first he thought her nudity was a trick of the night. Then when he realized it was no trick, when his mind registered what his eyes had seen, when his body caught up, he knew that whatever past satisfaction he'd felt with Marcie or any other woman was a dismal substitute for the possibilities with Keely.

He had wanted to reach out and draw her close. Wrap her wet braid around his hand, taste her mouth and fit himself into her body.

And then she'd seen him.

Her reaction had pleased him enormously, but then it shouldn't have surprised him. She didn't blush. She didn't screech like some outraged virgin. She simply stood there.

He knew if he'd come off the railing, crossed the deck and touched her, he'd never have been able to deal with her on a day-to-day basis on the Island.

He let out a long breath and grimaced at the last swallow of coffee. Maybe Patsy was right. Maybe he had messed things up with Marcie. If he'd married her, then Keely Lockwood would still be only the little girl in the picture on her father's desk.

It promised to be a very long thirty days.

Chapter 4

Black Horse Island lay far enough off the coast of Rhode Island to discourage the most ardent swimmer. Before a privately funded youth organization purchased the onetime haven for wild horses and turned it into a refuge for troubled boys, it had barely garnered a glance from passing boats. Roughly the shape of Tennessee, it comprised eighty acres. Its trees, stony terrain, even the wild roses that tangled amid the beach grass and rocks, were regarded as untamable by the few developers who'd considered the Island a viable piece of real estate.

The wild atmosphere had convinced Keely's father to take the directorship. He wanted to demonstrate to every boy who went through the four-month program that structure in their lives led to direction and a feeling of self-worth, which they should seek even under the most unworkable circumstances.

In a contract with Rhode Island, and patterned after a juvenile training school but without the bars and escape-proof fences, Black Horse Island became the state's alternative to jail for young male offenders who otherwise would have been sent to the Rhode Island Training School for Boys. If they completed the program successfully, they were given probationary freedom for another six months, and then released with a clean record.

The wind sighed in the trees as the ferry maneuvered into the wooden slip. The captain pumped three times on the horn to announce their arrival.

Keely stepped onto the dock, carrying her briefcase. The virginal environment was uncluttered by social sounds or civilized smells. The pungent odor of seaweed was strong as the July breeze suddenly shifted downwind. Sea gulls cawed above.

During the few months she'd lived on the Island as a child, Keely had developed a friendship with the ocean. Its timeless ebbing and rising of water soothed her; its presence a few feet from her beach house, and not the beach itself, was what had drawn her there after the divorce.

A euphoric anticipation swelled through her now. Dad, she thought, this is right, this is where I belong. This is always where I felt the closest to you.

The ferry was unloaded, with Jed directing the dispersal of food, supplies, mattresses and their personal things. Seth walked down the dock toward Keely. His commanding presence stemmed from his seeming to be one with the Island. At sixty-three, he was a man who'd found his spot and claimed it, and Keely had no doubt that he desired to die here on Black Horse.

He was dressed in old chinos and a faded flannel shirt he wore summer and winter. His face displayed the familiar calm and thoughtful attitude that seemed to sum up the principles her father had established: there will be no double standard here, no peer pressure, no social isolation.

''Seth, hello,'' Keely said, coming into his welcoming arms and finding herself fighting back sudden tears.

His big hand patted her back just as it had when she was a child. His voice was gruff and a little tight. ''Keely-kid, sure is good to see you here,'' he murmured, using the endearment that was almost as old as she.

It brought back the days when Seth took her fishing and listened to her rhapsodies about the boy on the football team she was sure she'd love forever. But the most poignant memory was of Seth looking cramped in a blue suit at her father's funeral. His big hands clasping and unclasping, his voice breaking, he'd said, ''I'm gonna miss him, Keely-kid.''

''It's as though Dad was still here,'' she said now, knowing he was there in spirit. Her gaze absorbed the swaying trees and the raw terrain.

''Me and the staff, we been working like beavers to get the place in shape. The bureaucratic do-gooders got it too civilized and then let the last batch of boys ruin it with their basic animal natures.'' His bushy eyebrows bunched in a scowl, then smoothed out as he extended his hand toward Jed. ''Sure am glad you changed your mind.''

Jed, Keely noted, didn't explain his earlier reluctance. ''Seth, you old codger, you're getting soft. When I was here, you and the Judge made sure we checked our basic animal natures here at the dock.''

"We sure did. You and Keely-kid will get things back the way they used to be," he said confidently.

Keely was about to remind Seth that she and Jed were not partners, but there was plenty of time to sort out roles and responsibility. And Seth's obvious relief at seeing Jed added to her decision to remain silent. She knew Seth adhered to the axiom that the men worked and the women worried. The fact that he saw her and Jed as partners was an enormous step.

As they walked up the beach to the cleared section of the Island, Keely found herself facing the enormity of her responsibility—turning difficult kids around to lead productive lives.

Jed and Seth walked ahead of her, discussing the new generator that needed to be enclosed. She let them walk on toward the main building, which housed the office, a small classroom with a library and the kitchen and eating area. The staff who worked on the Island full-time, including Seth and Marvin, the middle-aged Mr. Fixit, had cabins that sat to the left of the main building. Irma occupied the loft above the kitchen.

Keely walked across the clearing a few hundred feet to another row of cabins. The one she would occupy was a square wooden-framed structure with an enormous beehive hanging from one corner of the roof. Bees swarmed dangerously close to the only entrance, and she envisioned herself having to calculate as to the safest way to duck into and out of the cabin. She made a mental note to ask Jed to get rid of the hive.

There was a cabin for each of the boys. Her father believed privacy was one of life's most precious pleasures, and the majority of kids who came to the Island had never lived where they had any privacy. The walls were wooden and rough. The furniture in each cabin consisted of a scratched but newly painted dresser, a small table and chair and a bed frame awaiting one of the new mattresses that would replace the hacked and burned ones left by the last occupant. Serviceable furniture, not spectacular, but Keely knew each boy would bring his own personality, and within a week the rooms would be as individual as the kids.

"The place hasn't changed much since I was here."

Keely whirled around. She'd been so engrossed in her inspection of the last cabin that she hadn't heard Jed approach. He stood to her left, one duffel bag slung over his shoulder, the other on the ground next to what looked like a roll of canvas. Her own things had been placed in front of her cabin. The wind ruffled his hair, and he raked it back with the hand that wasn't holding a can of soda.

Keely waved away a bee. She slipped her hands into her jumpsuit pockets, wishing she could forget the last time she'd seen Jed with a can of soda.

He'd virtually ignored her since they left the diner. After ensuring that all the gear headed for the Island was loaded, he'd taken her arm and guided her firmly on board the ferry, making her feel like one of his duffel bags. He'd left her standing at the railing while he mumbled something about seeing the captain.

He was obviously irritated, and she sensed it was more with himself than with her. She'd done enough counseling to know that his reluctant confession about Patsy, followed by the mention of Marcie, had rattled his usual control.

Now she watched him roll the cold can across his forehead. "I hope Turk and the other kids appreciate the chance they're getting. Coming here is a sure sight better than being tossed in the state training school."

"You were there, weren't you? Before you came to the Island."

"Yeah, a few times," he said in a way that made those times seem distant and gratefully forgotten. "Privacy and the taste of freedom make the Island different. The training school is closed in, with smells, noise and—" he glanced over at Keely, and she was sure she saw traces of anger "—zero privacy. They read your mail, listen in on phone calls and generally make you feel invaded."

She felt at a loss for words. Saying she understood would be ridiculous. "The Island must have seemed like a paradise after that."

"Paradise and then some." He offered her the soda. "Want a sip?"

Again she was reminded of the night before, of Jed sitting on the railing holding the can. "No thanks." She stepped away from him and started toward her cabin.

Jed walked with her and stopped halfway between the boys' cabins and hers. He studied the area with a carpenter's eye, looking first at her cabin and then at the others. "The tent should fit here with plenty of room to spare."

Keely frowned. "What tent? What are you talking about?"

"Where I'm sleeping. Or did you expect your male presence to work twenty-four hours a day?"

She heard the sharpness in his words. It didn't cut like a knife, and seemed to have been caused more by impatience. "I assumed you would sleep with Seth. He mentioned that to me when we first discussed you coming. In fact, he had an extra bed moved in for you."

He unrolled the green canvas and laid out the tent poles. "But no one discussed it with me," he said easily. "I don't like sleeping with other people."

Does that go for women, too? The question jumped into her mind with a disturbing quickness. Watching him unfold the soon-to-be tent, she pinched her mouth shut to make sure no awkward comment escaped. After her query about his sleeping with Patsy, she intended to stay as far away as possible from any discussion that could lead to her asking questions that were none of her business.

"So you intend to pitch a tent. How resourceful."

He glanced up at her from a hunched-down position. His eyes looked soft and mellow, holding her with unsaid possibilities. Then, as though all those possibilities were only in her imagination, he grinned with what she thought was a touch of playfulness.

"Resourcefulness is one of my better traits."

Later, while she was putting her clothes away in her cabin, she heard him pitching the tent outside.

She peeked out the window and, to her total disgust, found that she was more interested in the fluid movement of his body than in his tent-erecting expertise. His black hair was held back by the red bandanna he'd tied around his head to catch the sweat. He'd taken off his shirt, and Keely was fascinated with the pull and ripple of taut skin over hardworking muscles.

Muscles were a necessity for a carpenter. But did he view having them as a way of attracting women? Not Jed Corey, she decided.

He wore no belt on his jeans and didn't even seem in the least concerned that they rode low on his hips. As her eyes skimmed the waistband, she realized something and took a deep, shuddering breath. He wasn't wearing any underwear. She kept blinking, trying to see some strip of white, knowing if he wore them, they'd be white cotton briefs. Designer underwear on Jed was as likely as snow in July.

The final tent peg was in, and when Jed walked around testing each pole for sturdiness, she saw the scar low on his belly. White against his deeply tanned skin. Even with the distance between them, she was able to note that it traveled a ragged road. She stared at it with a strange fascination, wondering how close he'd come to dying and who had cut him. An odd jumble of feelings she didn't recognize churned inside her.

She turned away from the window, leaned against the wall and crossed her arms tightly in front of her. It seemed that whenever she encountered Jed she learned something new.

She wondered how old he was when he got the scar. She wondered if anyone wept for him. A mother, a friend, a girlfriend.

She heard Seth call Jed from the clearing, and a few of the other staff members yelled welcome. She recognized Marvin's voice saying he was glad Jed was here.

Keely realized that she, too, from more than a professional perspective, was glad Jed had come to the Island.

After she finished putting her clothes away, she made up the single bed with fresh sheets and the lightweight blue quilt she'd brought from the beach house. In the tiny bathroom, she showered, and with shampoo dripping over her eyes, she realized suddenly why Jed had pitched his tent beside her cabin.

Protection.

Protecting Keely had been her father's reason for in-sisting, with her mother's agreement, that the Island was no place for a young girl. She'd resented it then; now she felt a tiny kernel of security, a reaction to Jed that she didn't want to feel.

But even worse was the more revealing realization: that prior to meeting Jed, she'd felt insecure.

She rinsed her hair, squeezing out the water. He could have made some pronouncement about why he'd come to the Island, or warned her again about Turk. In-stead, he'd calmly drunk from the soda can, talked a little about his past and without any fanfare pitched the tent.

She searched in her mind for even a trickle of resent-ment. When she found none, she realized that his being there had nothing to do with protecting her from Turk or the others, but with protecting her need to continue her father's dream.

The rest of that day and the next morning were spent getting ready for the arrival of the boys. The new mat-tresses were put in place. Keely double- and triple-checked the food supply, with Irma assuring her they had enough. Jed sorted the sports equipment and even repaired a leaky rowboat for fishing. Keely made the classroom schedule. She knew each boy would prefer fishing with Jed to sitting over a textbook, but she in-tended to make the learning process a part of their everyday lives.

In the small, but functional office a few hours be-fore the ferry was due to arrive, she set up her counsel-ing appointments, placing Turk's name first. Then she leaned back in the squeaky chair and took off her glasses. Despite the trees and the ocean nearby, the wind was hot and the air stuffy. Ninety degrees, Irma had complained at breakfast—too hot to cook. But she'd appeared a few moments ago with a plate of zucchini-and-nut bread.

The zucchini came from the large garden that Seth and the staff tended every year. The vegetables had miraculously escaped damage during the rampage of vandalism. Irma had also made a pot of coffee and set it on the filing cabinet. Keely knew that despite the heat, Seth liked to drink coffee, and Irma catered to Seth as she did to all the males who went through Black Horse.

The preliminary report to Judge Nelson and the Crisis board that she needed to finish lay on her desk. She put her glasses on top, deciding that even on an island she couldn't escape paperwork.

She plucked her blue T-shirt away from her body, wishing she could shed it and her shorts and skinny-dip by Pirate's Den on the far side of the Island.

Sighing away that thought, she turned her chair toward the open window and curled her bare feet over the edge of a bottom desk drawer that was slightly ajar. Jed was outside going over a load of lumber that had arrived on the first ferry this morning. He intended to include all the boys in the building of the generator's house.

Keely was allowing her mind to form an irrational hope that Jed would take off his shirt again, when Seth stepped into the office.

"Got a message for you from a woman named—" Seth fished in his pocket and took out a crumpled piece of paper "—Barbara Isherwood? Didn't ring any bells, but she said she wanted to talk to you."

Keely frowned. Barbara Isherwood was a tenacious real estate agent who saw every buyer as a future seller.

Needs change and clients move upscale, she'd told Keely when she'd sold the beach house. Before Keely had finished with the closing, Barbara was handing her a business card and saying, when you decide to sell, call me.

"She probably thinks she can make a killing on the beach house," Keely said, thankful there were no phones on the Island. They stayed in touch with the mainland and the coast guard through a marine radio.

Seth handed her the slip of paper, which revealed no more than what he'd said. She tossed it into the trash, then glanced out the window in time to see Jed lift a two-by-four to another stack.

The house for the generator would be built right outside her office window, giving her an undisturbed view of the progress. Her pleasure, she told herself, had nothing to do with the undisturbed view she'd have of Jed. As her thoughts traveled down that road of sensual discovery, she dropped her feet to the floor and slammed the drawer closed. Her body felt flushed, and she deliberately swung the chair so that she faced Seth.

"Zucchini bread," Seth said with a lick of his lips. "Irma's been busy." He broke off a corner from a thick moist slice and popped it into his mouth.

"She's going to be even busier once the kids arrive." Keely's gaze sought out Jed again, and her voice was pensive when she asked, "Seth, what was Jed like when he was here?"

Seth licked crumbs from his finger. "A hell-raiser."

Keely allowed herself the tiniest of grins. "That tame, huh?"

"Hey, it's no wonder."

He poured himself a mug of coffee, then offered to do the same for her. After she shook her head, showing him the soda she was drinking, he helped himself to more bread.

"The kid lived on the streets after his mother died. Most of what anyone knows about her came from the neighbors. Jed never talked about her. Drank herself into a boozy oblivion. Jed must have been about seven or so."

"Seven years old?" Keely stopped her soda can halfway to her mouth. Seven was the age of wonder and discovery, of still believing in Santa Claus and the tooth fairy. "What about his father? Other family members?" When Seth shook his head, she felt a grinding pain deep inside. "Then where was the state?"

"They tried. They couldn't find him. You know how the street can become the parent, the role model? Jed learned and he practiced. He had quite a reputation for car theft and a temper so hot it could melt steel. He'd been here less than an hour when he broke all the furniture in his cabin."

Keely sat forward. Images of Jed Corey out of control simply would not form, yet she knew Seth wasn't exaggerating. She was still reeling from the thought of a seven-year-old living on the street. "What did Dad do?"

Seth chewed a mouthful of bread, stopping to feel a tooth when he hit one of the nuts. He washed down the food with his coffee, then said, "Nothing. He told Jed he hoped Jed would get a good night's sleep on the pile of firewood he'd created." Seth leaned back in a barrel chair, his voice lower. "That made Jed use language the likes of which I haven't heard since. Your father didn't budge. He gave Jed a lot of rope until the day Jed threatened to kill him."

Keely paled. "My God. Dad never told me about that."

"Probably never told Rosemary, either. Edgar was real careful about saying too much to either of you. Didn't want you worrying."

Keely bit back the retort on her tongue. Didn't want them to worry? Didn't her father know that she and Rosemary worried more because of his silence and vague answers whenever either of them probed too much into the inner workings of the Island. She recalled her mother telling her that when Jed came to see her after the funeral he'd shared some very personal things with her. Was threatening to kill the Judge one of them?

"Jed wouldn't have done it," Seth said as though reassuring her that she had nothing to fear from the Jed of today. "It was a last-ditch effort to hang on to the only code he knew—kill or be killed. I think in your father he saw all the things he didn't have and he resented it. Sort of similar to killing the messenger because you don't like the message."

Kill or be killed. Keely shivered. She wanted to ask Seth if Jed had ever killed anyone, but she wasn't sure she wanted to know. Of course he hadn't, she told herself. Seth would never have persuaded the board to allow a killer to come to the Island.

Seth looked out the window where Jed was still working.

"I'll never forget it," he said softly. "The other kids had gathered around to see who'd win. Jed represented a sort of screw-you-and-strut-your-stuff attitude, while the Judge was the authority figure. Your dad was smart. He knew that Jed would turn or burn that afternoon.

Jed had a knife. Instead of looking around for help, the Judge told everyone to leave."

Keely felt adrenaline storm through her body. Was that how Jed had got the scar? Had her father somehow wrestled the knife away and cut him? For some insane reason she didn't like that idea any more than her father's being the victim.

"When your father told me about it later, I cried like a baby. Here was Jed, those gray eyes as cold as a February moon, and your dad scared but knowing he couldn't back down.

"Anyway, he looked at Jed and said, 'Let me have the knife. You can't win this one, and if you kill me, you'll go to prison.'"

Keely found herself amazed that her father could have been so rational, but then that was what had made him so successful with the kids.

Seth continued. "Jed stared him down and finally said, 'No one will give a damn.'" Seth cleared his throat. "Then his language got a little too blue to repeat, Keely-kid."

"It's still a little blue on occasion," she said, remembering the conversation in the diner about Patsy.

"Your dad never blinked. He waited until Jed got finished, and then he told him he gave a damn about him. That was why Jed was here. Yep, Edgar looked straight into those cold gray eyes and told him if he didn't get himself straightened out while he was here on the Island, the terror that lived inside him would eat him alive."

Seth walked to the window, blocking her view of Jed. "It might have been your dad seeing through all the hard shell, or it might have been some core inside Jed that believed him. Whatever it was, Jed handed over the knife. Watching him now, knowing what he was and how far he's come... I'll tell you, Keely-kid, it's enough to make me believe there's hope for the kids coming today."

A few weeks ago, she would have breezily said, of course there's hope. Today, she realized that to get to the hope, she would have to dig through the terror.

A half hour before the boys were due to arrive, Keely excused herself to spend a few minutes alone, trying to get her nervousness under control.

In her cabin, she changed clothes. Blotting her face with a cold washcloth, she peered at herself in the mirror. This isn't some vital pass-or-fail test, she thought. But she knew it was. Not the arrival of the kids, but the short amount of time she had in which to prove that she was as capable as her father. Thirty days; a lifetime if she messed up. She desperately wanted to give the boys what they hadn't found at home, what the street would always deny them—hope and promise, a chance to believe in themselves and make serious choices about the future.

"Keely? The ferry is pulling in."

Jed stood in the doorway. His hair was combed, and he wore a soft chambray shirt and jeans not worn enough yet to be patched. He looked a little uncomfortable, as though he didn't want to venture into her cabin. A haunting picture of a seven-year-old Jed not having anyplace to go and knowing no one wanted him made her heart break. Just as the promise of the man had lived in the boy, Keely knew that the pain of that boy still lived in the man.

"Hi. Come on in."

"Hollywood might be persuaded to do a sequel to *The Killer Bees*," he said as he ducked from a determined insect diving at his neck.

She grinned. "I know. I was going to ask you to take it down for me."

He peered at the hive with little enthusiasm. "How about if I build you another entrance to the cabin?"

"That would be easier?"

"Let's just say I respect their right to swarm and live undisturbed." He closed the screen door and suddenly looked leery, as if he'd crossed into uncharted territory.

"I'm almost ready." She'd finally decided to wear jeans. A skirt seemed too formal and shorts too revealing. She took a deep breath and flipped up the collar of her light green cotton shirt. Above her left breast was the Black Horse logo. She gave her braid a final inspection and was about to turn around when Jed's words stopped her.

"Don't move," Jed said in a low voice as he stepped to where she stood by the dresser. His hand brushed over the crown of her head, down her braid. Then his fingers curled into a fist and he flung something to the floor and stepped on it. "A bee."

"In my hair?"

"He must have come in when I opened the door. They're attracted to perfume."

"I'm not wearing any— Oh. The violet splash."

"Yes, the violets."

Perhaps it was the way he said it that made her breath catch. As though violets scenting and clinging to her were a fact he'd known and treasured, yet found disturbing. The loud buzzing in her ears had nothing to do with the bees outside.

He touched the spot on her hair where the bee had been, then searched down the braid, coil by coil.

She gulped, afraid to look into the mirror, knowing his eyes watched her, wanting for the first time since her divorce to feel the damp caress of a man's mouth against her neck. Her mind scrambled for some subject, any subject that would break the tension. "I wanted to ask you," she said, running out of breath on the third word.

He wound a wisp of hair around his finger. "Ask me what?"

To kiss me, Jed. To touch me. To quench this growing ache when you're near me. His touch confused her reasoning, and she gulped again.

"The beehive." Stupid, she thought, we've already talked about the beehive.

"I'll take care of it."

"When?"

"Tonight."

"When it's dark?"

"Whenever you want me to."

She closed her eyes, finding no relief in the blackness behind her eyelids. Her body felt hot and tight and eager—for him, for his hand to slide around her neck, for his words to be muffled against her skin.

Then as though he knew and decided to deny her, he stepped away. Keely felt the chill of his withdrawal, and shivering, she groped for a sense of balance. Jed touched her arm in a steadying gesture. He was breathing deeply.

She started toward the door, almost welcoming the sight of the bees. She never made it. His hand slipped around her neck to gently stop her.

Slowly he wound the braid loosely around his wrist, as though he were connecting them. He turned her around to face him, heading off any attempt at escape. Then he stared down at her, his eyes blazing with erotic promise.

His hand caressed her hair, urging her head to tip back so that she felt his breath on her mouth. "Tell me this doesn't make any sense. Tell me to go away, Keely."

Instead of answering him, she wet her lips, not to be provocative, but because she needed to. It was good that he held her, because she was sure her knees had given up any idea of support since he'd touched her.

The hand not tangled in her braid held her hip, drawing her to him. "Ah, babe, there's no denial in your eyes," he murmured a second before his mouth closed over hers.

Had a woman ever fainted from a kiss? Keely felt light-headed and parched. His lips pressed and coaxed. His tongue burned and branded her with a heat so hot she thought she would catch on fire. She yearned for more, and wound her arms around his neck.

He groaned as their bodies settled together, breasts to chest, hardness to softness. She wiggled, murmured his name and tightened her arms. When she finally felt him hard and heavy against her, he set her away from him.

With his head back, his breathing raspy, he raked both hands through his hair, keeping them there as though he were holding his body in one piece.

Keely sat down on her bed, feeling as though she'd barely survived a catastrophe. Had she really allowed herself to kiss him like that? As though being apart from him would be worse than dying?

"I knew I shouldn't have come in here," Jed muttered in a hoarse voice.

"I invited you in."

"Yeah, you and the bees."

"Look, don't beat yourself up about it. It was only a kiss. Men and women kiss all the time. It doesn't mean a relationship. It's not like there could ever be anything between us."

"Right. I'm not your type and I don't want to be."

"Exactly. I blame myself, too. You're very different than any of the men I've known, and I suppose that makes you interesting to me."

"Like an odd specimen you might find in some dark alley, huh?"

"Don't put words in my mouth."

His eyes darkened, and the lines in his face deepened. "You know damn well that's not what I want to put in your mouth."

The response that popped into her mind invited danger—and a slow unraveling of some knotted truth. The men Keely had dated since the divorce flirted boyishly, and sexual overtones were always veiled in proper smiles. There was nothing boyish or proper about Jed. Had she always settled for men like Paul, men who were safe, men who were really boys?

Jed was different, that was all. A few moments ago, hadn't she told him that was why she found him interesting?

She heard the screen door unlatch. "Jed?"

"It wasn't only a kiss. That's the problem," he said, and she knew whatever control he'd lost was now firmly back in place.

The ferry horn pumped three times. Without a backward look, he walked out, letting the screen door slam shut.

She sighed and stood. These feelings running hot and thick through her were disturbing, not because she had them, but because they kept getting stronger and harder to ignore.

She had no room in her life to nurture a relationship with a man. Unlike Paul, Jed had made independence a priority, but she knew men in general liked attention. Paul had craved it to the point where she'd finally told him she wasn't his mother and to grow up.

When her father had been home, her mother had fallen all over herself to be available. Even Irma fussed over Seth, and although he feigned indifference Keely knew he loved it.

She fisted her hands, trying to ignore the hot promise Jed had sealed on her mouth. She didn't like the twist her thoughts were taking. That Jed probably wanted attention wasn't what bothered her; it was his determination to ignore her.

"Damn you, Jed Corey. Damn you."

As she stood on the dock and watched the ferry nestle into the slip, Keely found herself still musing over what had happened in the cabin. She could still feel Jed's body pressed against hers, and taste his mouth, hot and tingly, over her lips.

She straightened her shoulders and raised her chin. Thank God, there was a no-sex rule on the Island. One thing she was very sure of: the Island would succeed again, and she intended to be right here to help it along.

She glanced to her left where a few feet away, Jed and Seth were deep in conversation. Marvin, Irma and the rest of the staff fanned out to welcome the new arrivals. The boys scuffed off the ferry, their walk as much of a challenge as the expressions on their faces.

The kiss in the cabin was an aberration, Keely decided with cool logic. A perfectly normal reaction of two people stranded away from everyone else their age. The boys would keep them both too busy to be thinking about go-nowhere intimacies.

Chapter 5

Hey man, where are the black horses?"

"Ain't no black horses, Snakeman. They ain't even got a broad to ride on this place." His brown hair was shaved on one side, and one ear flaunted a gold earring. Dressed in camouflage green, unlaced high-top sneakers and a cocky smile, he wasn't the first one off the ferry, but there was no doubt he was the leader. His voice carried an edge of authority, and the others responded to his comment with raucous laughter peppered with a few obscene remarks.

When Turk Solitto swaggered over to Keely, all of Jed's protective instincts sprang to alert. Turk grinned up at her with enough pure lust to cause Jed's fingers to clench.

"Except you, baby," Turk whispered with a street-tough leer. "You here for us to ride and tame?"

One thought rode in Jed's mind, and he gave it free rein. Lay one hand on her, kid, and you'll answer to me.

Keely regarded Turk coolly. Jed was reminded of that day in his apartment when he'd felt like the intruder. As she had then, she didn't back down. She displayed no nervous gestures. He unclenched his hands, allowing them to relax.

Seth started forward and Jed stopped him. "Let her handle him," Jed said in a low voice.

"I don't like him talking to her that way."

Jed squeezed the older man's shoulder. "It's only words. Keely knows that."

With a sigh of confirmation rather than a question, Keely said, "You must be Turk."

Turk strutted around in a circle as if he'd won a contest. "Hot damn! She knows me. My rep has gone and laid the way for my arrival."

"A stunning one, too," Keely said with a hint of amusement in her voice. She hadn't moved, giving him plenty of room to get his bearings.

"Yeah, you think so? Wait till you see me in real action."

Jed took a step forward.

Seth muttered, "It's about time."

The other kids, all of whom were behind Turk, snickered. Snakeman let go of a stuffed pillowcase he was carrying, and dropped on it as though he expected to be there a while.

Keely never took her eyes off Turk. "How about right now?"

"Huh?"

"Action, Turk. Let's see what you can do. We can start by you handing over the padlock on your duffel before it finds its way into a sock."

He blinked, then swallowed, and Jed was sure he saw a rough respect for Keely in the boy's eyes. Turk looked her over, his cocky smile shrinking. "You know about locks and socks?"

Jed allowed himself a moment of pride in her. He hadn't thought she'd paid much attention to him when he laid out the facts about Turk. But she had, and she was handling herself like a pro.

"Uh-huh, and about bats and ice picks," Keely replied in a matter-of-fact voice. "Sometimes you even rely on your fists."

Turk squinted. Jed doubted the fifteen-year-old remembered the last time a female had stood up to him.

"This lock, you know, it's like my good luck charm," he cajoled, sidling up to Keely as if they were street buddies who'd gone down together a few times.

Keely folded her arms and slowly shook her head.

"Hey, my life could be hangin' in danger here. You wouldn't want me to get killed, would you?"

"I'm going to make every effort to keep you alive," Keely replied solemnly.

"Yeah, but if I had my good luck charm here, you'd hardly ever have to watch me."

"That's what I'm afraid of."

"Hey, what if I give you my socks?" His sudden boyish grin reeked with the sincerity of a con artist. "I got lots of socks you can have. That way the lock will be like, uh, useless, you know?"

Keely shifted her weight, stared at him long enough to kill his grin and then held out her hand. "The lock, Turk."

Jed was amazed. Turk cursed and dropped the bag, obviously aware that authority was being established. Jed had never doubted Keely's gutsiness, but he hadn't expected her to zero in on Turk before the kid was on the Island for ten minutes. Maybe this dream of hers was a possibility.

Turk tossed the lock to Keely, his look cold enough to freeze the sun. A few more colorful words spewed out of him before he picked up the duffel bag and swung it over his shoulder, wincing and then swearing.

Wisely, Keely said nothing. The bag weighed him down considerably.

Snakeman came to his feet smoothly but slowly, like a lethargic reptile, retrieved his pillowcase and with the others fell into place behind Keely and Turk. Seth stayed behind to talk to the ferry boat captain. Irma went back to the kitchen and the rest of the staff went about their duties.

Keely took the boys to her office, checked them all in and then accompanied them down to the cabins. Turk stopped by the tent and Jed stayed a few feet behind Keely. Turk had yet to acknowledge that he knew Jed, but Jed knew he was waiting for the right time—preferably a time when Turk had the upper hand or at least wouldn't be in danger of looking weak in front of the others.

Undaunted by Keely's winning the first round, Turk dropped one arm around her neck. "Hey, baby, I want the tent. You and me, we can, uh, get somethin' goin'."

Keely didn't move away or make any attempt to get his arm off. Jed scowled, tried to count to ten but only made it to five when Turk bent his head toward her ear.

"Get your hands off her, Solitto."

Turk cocked his head back. Jed's sharp look sliced into him.

Snakeman quit digging a hole in the dirt. Everyone fell suddenly silent. Keely looked back at Jed, her expression neutral.

Turk slowly removed his arm. "Chill out, man. I ain't one to cruise unless the broad is willing." The words were tough, but Jed let them stand. He'd made his point.

Keely swatted at a bee that buzzed in front of her face. "Jed has the tent," she said, and ducked when another bee flew over her head.

Turk grinned a cocky grin. "You scared of a little bee?"

"Terrified," she said without so much as a smile.

Jed chuckled to himself. She was appealing to Turk's male instincts to protect. First she disarmed him, and then when he was thinking he had her all figured out she went all female on him.

With a swat that Jed thought better suited to the street, Turk killed the bee. After volunteering to remove the hive from Keely's cabin, he, along with the rest of the boys, began to move his stuff into the cabins.

For the next hour she made sure everyone was settled and collected an assortment of things that could be lethal. She also informed them that dinner was at five.

While Jed waited for her, he leaned against a nearby maple tree. When it was obvious she was going to talk to each kid individually, he slid down to the ground and stretched out his legs.

He looked at the beehive, giving in to the prick of annoyance that the task of its removal had been handed to Turk. She was giving orders, handing out duties and generally doing quite well without him.

Too well, he thought. He had to admit that the stereotype of a woman in need of a protector had not applied to Keely. He'd begun to enjoy the role—or had he created the role because she disturbed him? Or fascinated him? Or turned him on?

He'd kissed her to prove she was just like any woman who smelled good. He'd kissed her to prove to himself he could hunger and walk away. He'd kissed her to prove she wasn't going to be anywhere near as sensational as he'd imagined.

Like hell.

He'd kissed her because sweet madness was preferable to the ragged edges of frustration. What had happened to his easy dismissal of a woman? What had happened to the loner who enforced solitary existence on himself to keep away pain and rejection?

Rejection by a mother who preferred booze to a small boy had sent him to the street so many years ago. And despite the Judge's best efforts, despite the Judge's determination to never turn away a kid in trouble, the foundation of Jed's whole life—the belief that nobody wanted him—wouldn't come apart.

He closed his eyes to listen to nature gossip and whisper around him. These were the sounds of life and energy and hope, sounds he'd never heard until he came to the Island at sixteen. He took a deep breath and watched a sparrow flutter from one tree limb to another, teetering and yet keeping its balance.

Like the sparrow, Jed had experienced teetering, then balance. That had been his method also. He'd done okay. He wasn't in prison. He'd kept out of trouble. He'd even had some success by his own standard.

There was no woman, and anyone looking at his background would assume it had something to do with not trusting women or being afraid of rejection. But it was more than that. He knew the basic problem was his own. Rejection implied something or someone to reject. Giving of himself was dangerous. He thought of Turk, full of swagger and self-confidence—a kid growing into trouble. Not unlike himself when he was fifteen.

When he learned that control was his best defense against pain, rejection and disaster, he'd embraced it.

Until he'd found Keely Lockwood in his apartment.

Keely with her long braid, her spring-green eyes, her dream to make the Island a success the way it had been when the Judge was alive. Even her drill-sergeant efficiency intrigued him.

"Taking a nap, Jed?"

He opened his eyes to see her standing in front of him. Her legs formed an intriguing upside-down V. One of her hands twitched on her left hip. In her right hand, she grasped a plastic bag shaped as if it held a variety of trouble. He decided the bag was probably full of stuff she thought could be used as weapons.

Jed allowed his gaze to follow the inside seam on her jeans's left thigh all the way to the point of the V. His thoughts, he realized, matched Turk's earlier words about riding and taming.

He uncrossed his ankles. If he lifted one leg in a quick motion, she'd tumble into his lap. Now that idea had a lot of possibilities.

He had to tip back his head to meet her eyes. They glittered with a rich green color, and he thought of sparks dancing along a fuse to the waiting dynamite.

"Your strong male presence is worn out," he said.

"I want to talk to you."

"I'm listening."

"In my office. Now."

"Did anyone ever tell you you'd make a great drill sergeant?"

"Jed, I'm in no mood for any silly conversation. You and I have to come to an understanding as to who's in charge."

"Since you're holding that lethal-looking bag, it's hardly a debatable point," he replied, coming to his feet. "Okay, sarge. Lead the way."

She ignored him, stalking ahead of him, her back one long rigid line. She allowed the plastic bag to swing at her side, and Jed wisely kept his footsteps short enough to stay behind. He tried not to watch the sway of her hips, tried not to think about how they would fit against him.

Her braid bounced against her back, and Jed thought he should get a medal for control. He wanted to pull her back, lift her into his arms and carry her off to someplace private.

The old warrior mentality, he decided. It went right back to his days on the street, when claiming and owning turf was what life was all about. Back in the hellhole of existence.

But his curiosity played with what she would do. Would she struggle and scream? Would she strain to touch him with the passion he'd felt a few hours ago?

Priorities, Corey, he told himself. Get your priorities in order. Don't waste any more energy or logic denying you want to make love to her. That's as obvious as the sun. Doing is where the control counts. Doing it. Heavy and hard to her soft and willing.

He heaved a shuddering breath.

Hell.

Seth stood up when they walked into the office.

"Another message from the Isherwood woman, Keely-kid."

"Leave it on the desk, Seth. Would you excuse us for a moment?"

Seth glanced from Keely to Jed, who shrugged and rummaged in the small refrigerator for a soda. He snapped open a can of orange.

Seth said to Keely, "Yeah, sure. Got the kids all settled?"

"Yes," she replied, and Jed wondered how one word could sound so ominous. She walked over to her desk and dropped the plastic bag on top. "The chore lists need to be made up for laundry and garden work. Tell Irma to make sure the cleanup list for the kitchen is posted. I told the boys to check the bulletin board before they went to the table."

Seth cleared his throat. "Uh, Irma would prefer to do the dishes herself."

"Chores are part of the program, Seth. You know that and so does Irma."

"Yeah, but the last bunch broke more dishes than they washed."

"This isn't the last bunch."

"They're worse. And you shouldn't have let that Turk—or whatever he's called—talk to you the way he did. Respect for women is important. Your dad wouldn't have put up with it. Jed, you should have done something."

Jed knew that even though he agreed with Seth, this wasn't the time to say so. "Keely handled herself fine, Seth."

"I don't like it. An animal is what he is. He shouldn't be allowed to act like that."

Keely sighed, and her face softened. She slipped her arm through Seth's. "Turk isn't an animal. He's a kid with a lot of insecurities, and he deals with them by acting tough.''

Sounds familiar, Jed thought.

Keely continued. ''You of all people should know that. Turk used a lot of heavy words and dirty leers, but he didn't do anything.''

Seth patted her hand with fatherly concern. ''I wish your dad was here.''

Jed was struck by the emotion behind Seth's words. He wondered if Seth, too, wanted to recreate the Island as it had been when the Judge was in charge. And Seth's insisting that Jed be here was no doubt a protective gesture. Keely Lockwood seemed to bring out the protective instinct in the men in her life. He frowned at the realization that he'd included himself as one of those men.

''I wish he were here, too, Seth.'' She kissed his cheek.

Jed took a long swallow of the orange soda, thinking it would taste a lot better if it were beer.

After the door closed behind Seth, Keely glared at Jed. He was glad the plastic bag was on the desk.

''Jed.''

''I think I'll go with Seth.''

She stepped in front of the door and folded her arms over her chest. The gesture lifted her breasts just enough to distract him. ''A bad idea, huh?''

''You look like a little boy about to be punished.'' Then to his astonishment the color disappeared from her cheeks. ''You don't think I was too tough on them, do you?''

''On Turk and the rest? No.''

"So many of these kids grow up with emotional and verbal abuse. It simply isn't the way to try and help them."

"Keely, there's a difference between verbal abuse and not allowing them to intimidate you. They have to know who's boss and they have to follow the rules. Besides, kids respect you when you hold your ground like you did with Turk."

She walked over to the desk. He waited while she fussed with the reports, then read and frowned at the note Seth had left.

From the kitchen came the sound of clattering dishes. A whoop of laughter could be heard from the cabins.

Keely tucked a few strands of loose hair behind her ears and upended the plastic bag. Besides Turk's padlock, the contents included a rusty coat hanger folded up like a ruler, a door latch and a roll of wire.

Keely held up a potato peeler. "Do you know Tommy, the kid who had this, told me he brought it because he liked carrots?"

Her eyes flashed with indignation that anyone would think she was that stupid. Jed grinned.

"Did you get the beer out of Snakeman's pillowcase?" he asked.

"Beer?"

Jed arched his eyebrows.

"They had beer?" she asked with a squeak of outrage.

"It's called smuggling. Clever, aren't they?"

She rounded the desk and was starting out the door when he smoothly circled her waist with an arm and drew her around to face him.

"Don't bother. They popped those cans as soon as you were out of earshot."

She sighed. "What I'd like to know is why all this stuff wasn't taken from them before they got on the ferry."

"Keely, they got the stuff on the ferry. None of the things you collected are obvious weapons like a gun or a knife. What did you think they were doing during the ride over here? Looking at the passing boats and admiring the blue sky?"

"Damn," she muttered in a thoroughly disgusted tone. "I should have known."

"Listen to me. These kids spend their waking moments figuring angles. They don't cross a street without trying to outsmart the guy on the other side. You handled things fine today. And not finding the beer is a plus for you. This way, they might get careless because they'll figure you're not as savvy as they thought. And right now they think you're one savvy broad." She scowled, which he ignored. "That performance with Turk is being discussed right now, and all of them are trying to figure out how a woman could be so cool with Turk Solitto."

"This is like a game to them, isn't it?"

"Yes and no. They know this Island is their last hope, but street kids have more pride than brains at times. They don't want to be vulnerable, and so they'll act tough, while at the same time they don't want to be kicked out of here."

His hand was still on her waist, and when she made no motion to move away, Jed pressed his lips into her hair. It was a gesture of support rather than passion. He heard her sigh; then as if she'd suddenly become aware of him, she stepped away.

He dropped into a chair. Sliding down slightly, he placed his left ankle over his right knee. "You said you wanted to talk to me."

She'd walked over to her desk and methodically examined the cache of makeshift weapons. "Talk to you? Oh, yes, I did, didn't I?" She pressed her fingers against her temples and rubbed.

"Headache?"

"A little one."

She rubbed for another minute, and Jed concentrated on the scuff marks on his boot. Not as appealing as the shape of her mouth, but safer when his thoughts were headed toward the danger zone. His hands itched to settle her on his lap, to kiss away her stress and investigate the Black Horse logo that had the privilege of riding the crest of her breast.

"Why did you act so territorial when Turk put his arm around me? He wasn't going to hurt me."

"Hurting you wasn't the issue."

"I was handling things just fine."

"Not when he was about to tongue your ear."

Her cheeks flushed, and she quickly lowered her head. Jed waited, stamping down the urge to walk over to her and pull her into his arms. Despite her counseling abilities, despite her tough image, there were a few things she didn't know. Jed found that that increased his determination to protect her.

Finally she allowed her eyes to meet his.

"I didn't want you to be embarrassed."

She took a deep breath. "I should have known. I thought he was just going to whisper something. It would have ruined everything if I'd been embarrassed."

"At this point, yes. Turk wants to find a weakness, and if it's sexual he won't leave it alone."

"It was the way you did it, Jed." She peered at him as if poised for a disagreement. When he just shrugged, she said, "Ordering Turk to take his hands off me like you owned me... No, wait. Before you get angry, we need to settle exactly how we handle that sort of thing in the future."

"That sort of thing, Keely, is the reason I'm here."

"And just because I didn't know what he intended to do, you think I can't handle him."

"Don't get defensive. You handled him today because you caught him before he had a chance to figure you out. Don't underestimate him."

She had that soft spot for hurt creatures that the Judge had talked about.

"He's fifteen, Jed. He's got a lot of feelings he doesn't know how to deal with. Of course, he's going to swagger around like some macho stud. I told you that when I first asked you to come here."

He came out of the chair, planted both hands on her desk and leaned close enough to smell violets. "I don't want anything to happen to you. I owe that much to the Judge."

"I appreciate your loyalty to Dad, but you're treating me like I don't know what I'm doing."

"What about in your cabin, Keely? Did you know what you were doing then?"

To his surprise she met his question head-on.

"Yes, I knew exactly what I was doing. And you did, too. I'm not some ditzy female who gets herself into tough situations and then screams, blushes or faints. You're exactly like Turk. You've got this idea that women are space shots. But then you're all charm and sweetness when it comes to getting them into bed.''

He let his head drop forward, shaking it back and forth slowly. ''God,'' he muttered. He felt her hand in his hair, and he reared back as if she'd burned him.

''It was a twig,'' she said, showing him the small stick from the maple tree.

Their eyes met.

''Why do I want you?'' he asked quietly.

''Jed . . .''

''Answer me. Is it because you're beautiful? Is it because you smell so good? Is it because I want to unbraid your hair and spread it out on my belly?''

Instead of his voice getting louder with each question, it dropped lower. He sucked in his breath and swallowed the rest of his words, which had too much to do with the real reason why Turk's touching her made his gut grind. If anyone put his tongue in her ear, he wanted to make sure he was the one.

She moved away to stand by the window. Her shoulders trembled, and Jed cursed himself for saying as much as he did. The control he'd taken for granted for so many years had suffered a major crack.

''Look,'' Keely began, turning around to face him, her eyes wistful but determined. ''I have thirty days to prove I can handle things here. I have to take some reports over to Judge Nelson, and when I do I'll talk to him about getting someone to replace you. I know you only came out of obligation to my father, and I don't want to interfere in your life. If Judge Nelson gets right on it, he should be able to get someone in a couple of days.''

''No.''

Her expression was suddenly pleased and puzzled. "No?"

"I'm here and I intend to stay."

"And what about these, uh, feelings between us?"

"Can you keep your hands off me?"

Her chin came up; her eyes glittered. "Of course, I can."

"Then all we need to worry about is me."

And for the next three days, Jed worried about himself through nights without sleep and meals he barely tasted, but slowly the control limped back.

He watched her walk and told himself her legs were made for just that, not to wrap around a man's hips. He watched her eat and told himself her mouth was made for just that and not to bury his tongue in.

He listened to her using classroom techniques that made learning fun and visual, and told himself his own visual fun would stay in one of those hedonistic fantasies that galloped through his mind at the most inappropriate moments.

He sweated along with the kids to dig the foundation for the generator housing. They hand-mixed cement and poured it. Keely stood and watched, praising the kids and making Jed add one more layer of control.

He'd come to the conclusion years ago that when things looked as if they were going okay, they probably weren't. When the kids looked as if they were cooperating, they probably weren't. And when Keely thought she had all of them working together like industrious beavers, Jed knew something was going to mess things up.

"Hey, Turk, check that support beam to make sure it's been nailed tight," Jed called. He was standing outside what, if he closed his eyes and hoped, might eventually turn into an enclosure for the generator.

The building was a simple two-by-four shed. He'd drawn out the plans that way for two reasons. Complicated construction wasn't necessary, and his intent was to teach some basic carpentry techniques. The more elementary the framing and the closing, the easier it would be for the kids, whose use of hammers had been limited to engaging in vandalism.

"Hey Jed, you said we were goin' fishin'," one boy said.

"Later."

"When later?" Snakeman yelled.

"After we finish here."

"Man, I thought this place was goin' re-di-rect me," Turk shouted. "All I'm gettin' is calluses while you're gettin' free labor."

A chorus of "Yehs" and "You tell him, Turk" went up from the rest.

The air changed by not more than a whisper, but Jed detected it. He rolled up the plans he'd been studying, and crossed the grassless yard to where Turk stood. Despite the earring and the pimples that emphasized Turk's youth, Jed knew if he'd been the judge he would have sent the teenager off for about ten years of hard labor.

"Let's see the calluses."

"Huh?"

Jed ignored the hammer that dangled from Turk's hand. "Your hands, Turk, let's see them."

"I ain't a liar."

His voice got lower. "The hands."

"You callin' me a liar? You think you're so tough 'cuz you got the broad on your side. You get us guys out here on this pile of rock and sand, and you think you can abuse us, don't you?''

Jed felt a whiplash of fury inside him. "Turk?"

The youth lifted his chin to a cocky jut.

"Don't ever call Keely a broad again. Understand?" Jed said each word in a low ominous tone that brought not only Turk to silence but the rest of the boys also.

"Answer me!"

"Okay, yeah, okay," Turk said in a shaky voice.

Jed looked at each boy, waiting for the nod that indicated he, too, understood. When the last one responded, he said in a calm voice, "Good. Then let's get back to work."

Fifteen minutes later when they stopped for a break, Turk grumbled, "The rules here ain't no different than over there." Turk raised his soda can and gestured toward the mainland. "You get all the comforts like Keely in your bed— Hey, man, I didn't say broad." He gave a nervous laugh as though he expected Jed to explode.

Before Jed could say anything, the tense snickerings among the others shrank to uneasy chuckles.

Jed's mood darkened, not in disgust at Turk's remark, but at his own immediate reaction of wishing it were true. He took a breath and folded his arms over his chest.

One confrontation a day was enough, he decided. Although any relationship he had with Keely, business or personal, was no one's business, he recognized that the boys' assumption had merit. In their place he would have assumed the exact same thing.

And, he reminded himself, Turk and the others needed to see how much better things went when people kept their tempers under control.

"Okay," Jed said in a mild voice. "You guys want it straight?"

They looked at one another, obviously unsure about what kind of straight he was talking about, but too curious to walk away.

"I'm not her type." At this revelation, Jed saw that they were not only intrigued, but also beginning to give him their guarded acceptance.

"Yeah? Not her type?" At his grim nod, they all looked at him with a new respect.

"She blew you off, huh?"

"Keely's a class act. What can I say? I tried, but she says rules are rules."

"You mean you get no beer and no sex? Jeez."

"You got it."

"Hey man, that's a bummer. How come you're here when you don't have to be?"

"To teach you guys how to drive a straight nail."

They all laughed, the tension breaking. They tossed their soda cans into the trash, and Jed walked back to the roll of blueprints. Turk followed him.

"Jed?"

"Yeah?"

"I gotta see her later, you know, to tell her my whole life story."

"I think it's more of a conversation, Turk. Keely won't make you say any more than you want to."

"I ain't use to talkin' to bro—uh, I mean women." He gulped and Jed motioned him to go on. "'Cept my ma. And she gets, jeez, you know, all blubbery. Why don't I just tell you and you tell her, okay?"

"Turk, Keely's the counselor here."

"You did it at St. Mark's."

"That was more of a support group. And how would you know? You were never in one."

"I heard. Besides, who needs all that yakkin' and cryin'. Ain't nothin' but a bunch of babies. I ain't gonna say nothin' no matter what. A guy has a right to privacy, don't he? It's bad enough she took my lock. This is my private life we're talkin' about here."

"Turk, you're making too big a deal out of this."

He swallowed, looking vulnerable for the first time since he'd arrived on the Island. "There's things in my life, you know. Things that ain't nobody's business."

"I agree."

Turk's eyes widened. "Yeah? Like you got things in your life?"

The question was rife with amazement that an adult would agree with a kid. "You got it," Jed replied.

"And you ain't never told no one about them?"

"Keely's father. I told him."

"Yeah, I heard of him. Called the Judge. You told him, huh? What'd he do? Kick your ass out of here?"

Jed still had a vivid memory of when he'd threatened the Judge with a knife. "No. The Judge didn't believe in tossing punks out."

"Yeah, but she ain't the Judge. She's a girl."

"Woman, Turk." They were making progress, Jed thought. For the first time Turk hadn't said broad. "And how do you know she isn't? You haven't given her a chance." Then Jed decided to reverse the conversation. "I warned her about you."

His eyes filled with street-tough pride, and Jed had to work to stop his own smile when Turk's chest visibly expanded.

"Yeah? You told her about me?"

"That you were an SOB who liked to rip off old ladies."

"Hey man, I ain't never ripped off an old lady." His offense at the accusation made his voice rise to a squeaky pitch.

"Good. But you are tough."

Jed wasn't surprised when he saw Turk actually swagger. Toughness meant survival on the street, and a reputation such as Turk's went a long way to keeping you alive.

"Well, hell, you gotta be."

"Agreed. Now, how do you think it's gonna look to Keely if Turk Solitto, the tough man, won't even talk to her? I mean, I got a reputation here, too. I don't want to be accused of spreading lies and having her think I don't know what I'm talking about."

'Yeah, maybe you're right." He gave Jed a suspicious glower. "She ain't gonna make me tell her nothing I don't want to, right?"

"Right."

Turk strolled away, his chin up, his thumbs hooked into the belt loops of his jeans, his idea of male superiority intact.

Jed raked his fingers through his hair and glanced at the office window. He could see Keely was working.

Not a smart move, he thought grimly. He'd come to the Island to protect her from Turk, and what did he do? Blow an ideal way to keep her away from Turk.

It's not too late, he told himself. Walk into the office and tell her you had a long talk with Turk, and you think he'd be more comfortable speaking with you than her.

Keely was too good a counselor not to see the wisdom in that reasoning. In fact, Jed had no doubt she'd encourage Turk to talk to him. Not because she couldn't handle him, but because she'd want Turk to be comfortable.

That was part of the problem. Someone was always trying to make these kids comfortable when it came to assigning responsibility for their actions. It was too easy to blame broken families, lenient judges, poverty, peer pressure and so on. The list must have been compiled by the most imaginative social worker. Jed knew that telling every person in the system to shape up was a waste of breath.

Turk was a savvy kid, but Jed had seen a glimmer of hope a few minutes ago. Turk would change and come out stronger if he talked with Keely.

If he talked with Keely.

Jed let out a long breath that felt as if he'd been holding it for a lifetime. Is that what was happening to him? Was he changing as a result of Keely Lockwood? Not because he desired her. Not because she was the Judge's daughter and he felt an obligation to protect her. But simply because she'd come into his life?

On Turk and on himself, Keely was having an effect.

Their lives might not be as comfortable, Jed realized, but they would definitely be stronger.

Chapter 6

The following day, Jed knocked on the door to Keely's office. "You busy?"

Keely glanced up from where she was seated behind her desk, looking over reports on the Island. Why did he always look so sexy? His face was streaked with sweat. The red bandanna he'd worn when he pitched the tent and every day since then was anchored around his head, giving him a savage, primitive appeal that made her feel a little uncivilized for wanting to tame him. His T-shirt was light blue and untucked from jeans that had faded to almost white. She wondered if he knew jeans like his were selling at exorbitant prices in department stores.

Keely adjusted her glasses, grateful the fluttering in her stomach wasn't visible. She had to admit that in the past few days, they'd both done an admirable job of keeping all feelings between them strictly professional. When they laughed it was at one of the baseball games they both participated in with the kids. When they got serious it was over a problem one of the boys had. When they were alone they discussed the Island or some other topic, carefully avoiding personal comments or intimate looks.

"Actually, I'd welcome the interruption," she said, motioning him to come in. "I've reread these reports so many times, I'm beginning to think they should be rewritten." She took off her glasses.

"Is Nelson gonna read them while you wait?"

"He'll scan them to get a general idea of what we're doing. If they meet his approval, he'll begin nodding and say something like, 'You've made a good start,' which only means I won't get kicked out of here. Yet."

"How are the counseling sessions going?"

"Slow. But I didn't expect miracles. The kids are leery and I guess that's understandable."

"Turk?"

"Not too talkative, but we have lots of time."

"Ever the optimist." He took a can of orange soda out of the small refrigerator and popped the top. Keely watched as he tipped back his head, his throat muscles working greedily to drink down the cold liquid.

Lowering the can, he wiped the back of his hand across his mouth. "You look nice and cool and s—" He stopped himself at the last word, and she wondered if he meant sophisticated, snobbish or sexy.

She did look different today. She had dressed in a white cotton sweater with a rose screen-printed on the front and a pink gauzy cotton skirt, and arranged her hair in a loose figure-eight coil at the back of her head.

"Sensational."

"Oh," she murmured, his word not the one she expected, but infinitely more satisfying than the ones she'd considered. "Thank you."

He grinned at her then—a dangerous grin that told her he liked nudging her off balance and revealing himself in unexpected ways. He rubbed the cold can on one cheek.

"It's dusty and hot out there," he said, nodding toward the motionless trees. The sky was a clear blue; the cracked ground begged for rain to settle the dust.

He sprawled in a chair and stretched out his legs in front of him, wrists dangling over the chair arms. When he balanced the soda can on his buttoned fly, the fluttering in her stomach turned into a heavy, insistent pounding.

". . . to cool off."

Her gaze flew up to meet his. "What?"

"A couple of the staff are with the kids. They went swimming to cool off."

Which is what your thoughts need, she told herself. "You should have gone with them. You've been working practically nonstop since you began the house for the generator."

"There's an old saying about work keeping you out of trouble."

"Or playing getting you into trouble." She wasn't sure exactly why she said that. Jed regarded her with a strange look, as if he wasn't sure if she was teasing or serious.

Keely decided not to ask. "Did you want to see me about something in particular, Jed?"

He hesitated long enough to create a sizzle of expectation in Keely. "Not really. I was looking for a few moments of quiet. How long are you going to be gone?''

Will you miss me? she wondered, but didn't have the nerve to say it aloud. ''I'm not sure. I have to see Judge Nelson, and then I promised to meet a real estate agent.''

''For what?''

Keely sighed. ''Her name is Barbara Isherwood, and I don't know about what. She's called a couple of times. This morning when I talked to her, she said she wanted to discuss the matter in person. I agreed to meet her this afternoon mostly to get rid of her.''

''She must be hard up for sales if she's going to this much hassle. You ever talked to her before?''

''She sold me the beach house after my divorce, so I assume she wants to know if I'm interested in listing it since I'm here on the Island. She no doubt thinks I'm more likely to agree in person than via the marine radio.''

''You bought the beach house after your divorce,'' he said in a speculative voice, as if he were thinking aloud and trying to fit pieces of her past together. He was silent for a few moments, and she wondered if he expected her to add something. Something about her divorce? When she didn't, he said, ''You never have said much about your ex-husband.''

She'd slipped her glasses into the case. By habit, she raised the shield of defensiveness she'd created since the divorce; she felt wary. The divorce was history, nothing that could be changed, nor would she change it if she could. Only rarely did she think of Paul as her ex-husband; he was simply Paul Morrow, a lawyer with the attorney general's office. She'd recently heard he planned to marry again, and she wished him well. "Why would you want to know about Paul?"

"You said you bought the beach house after the divorce. I was just curious about why you were the one who moved."

"We had a condo in Providence. Paul loved it and I didn't, so the question of who got what was simple."

"Why did you get divorced?"

It was a question few people had asked her directly. She assumed they chose to think the four-year marriage simply hadn't worked. Most of the questions she asked herself had to do with why. Physical abuse, infidelity or even cultural differences would have been valid reasons, except none of them was true. To her, irreconcilable differences sounded like a cop-out akin to eating crackers in bed, or not putting the cap back on the toothpaste.

Jed, she decided as she watched him, probably wouldn't settle for too vague an answer.

"Because I didn't want to be married any longer. Paul had a thing about me staying home, and to put it bluntly, being his maid. We both decided that it was an unresolvable issue."

"A modern friendly divorce?"

"We still speak if that's what you mean."

He lifted the can and sipped. Then came the next question without any apology. "What about other men in your life? A boyfriend? Or is there more than one?"

Keely grinned at his directness. "Why, Jed Corey, what a personal question! Is this a safe sex question? Or are you trying to slot me into some category you've devised for the women you know?"

He didn't grin back—he scowled. Slowly she realized what he was really asking. A warm flush of satisfaction slid over her. Jed Corey's interest in her personal life was more than curiosity. She wasn't ready to believe the existence of a boyfriend would seriously bother him, but despite her own determination to not get involved with him, her femininity liked the idea of Jed being agitated.

"Forget it. It's none of my business," he growled, straightening up in the chair and crunching the empty soda can as if it were a piece of paper.

Keely sat forward. Having the upper hand with him was a rarity, and she had no intention of letting it get away.

With her hands folded on the desk as if she were a teacher getting ready to discipline an unruly student, she asked in her sweetest and calmest voice, "You think I'm going to see a man while I'm on the mainland, don't you? That's why you came in here."

"Aren't you?" He tossed the can, which sailed in a perfect arc into the trash can.

"What if I said yes? What if I said I'd made plans for a long night of lovemaking?" The minute the last word was out she regretted both questions.

He sucked in his breath as if it might be the last one he'd ever draw, and slowly got to his feet. "I gotta get back to work."

Suddenly Keely didn't feel so cocky. No doubt Jed was a man who enjoyed sex without having to look too long to find it. Here he was confined on this Island, forced to abstain, by his own choice she knew, but it was certainly not a choice most men would make. Teasing him about what a hot time she intended to have was the worst form of cruelty.

Certainly she owed him no explanation of her personal life, yet she didn't want him to think she slept around. Not only because she didn't, but also because she had a feeling Jed would hate it. Why his opinion of her mattered, she wasn't sure, but it did.

There's a double standard in there somewhere, she thought with a frown.

Jed was almost at the door.

Let him leave, she told herself. If he thought she had a boyfriend then he wouldn't bother her. She'd get through this trial period doing exactly what she'd come here to do—prove she was capable of taking her father's place.

Jed was here because of a bureaucratic decision. Once she established her credibility, he would no longer be needed. She'd handled the boys, and Turk hadn't been the trouble Jed had warned her about. Letting Jed leave her presence now would prove he simply worked here.

He meant nothing to her. His eyes didn't fascinate her. His past didn't make her curious. His control didn't tease at her to try to break it. Let him leave. Let him leave.

"Jed, wait."

He stopped.

"I'm sorry."

"For what? For planning on a long night of love-making?"

"For telling you I am when I'm not. There's no boy-friend or boyfriends. In fact, the last time I even had a date was, let's see..." She thought back over the past year. My God, she thought, I can't remember the last one I had. The reason was she simply didn't want to make the effort; neither did she want to get involved with anyone. She continued, "On second thought it was hardly a date. I had dinner with John McGovern, one of the members of the Children in Crisis board. That was in May. Two months ago."

No doubt Jed would think she was the pariah of the singles scene, she mused. However, no startled look was forthcoming from him.

He regarded her for a long, long time. His gray eyes were smoky and steady. Unblinking.

Finally he let his hand fall away from the door. "I owe you an apology," he said softly.

"Apology accepted."

"I had no right to ask you a question like that."

"And I shouldn't have been so flip with my answer."

"Friends?"

"I hope so."

He seemed to relax, coming forward and standing by the window. She heard his breathing settle into an even rhythm, and to her amazement it acted as a balm to her own erratic thoughts.

"I guess I did have something in mind when I came in here," he said finally. "Seth told me he'd given you a detailed description of what happened between your father and me. Why didn't you ask me about it?"

He didn't turn around, and his voice had no inflection. Was he amused? Angry? Guarded about her reaction?

She wet her lips while her mind filtered and sorted a dozen different answers.

Finally, she decided to be as straightforward as he had been in his comments about her divorce. "Because trying to get you to talk about yourself is frustrating. You dodge questions and avoid answers."

He shifted slightly, raising one arm and bracing his palm against the wall beside the window. His biceps bunched and bewitched her into wondering how casually she could touch him. Her fingertips tingled.

"A habit born of necessity," he replied, as if a tangled past had become simply a fact he lived with. "Most of the people who ask me questions have some ulterior motive. Everything from reforming me to nosiness."

"Maybe one of them asked because they cared about you."

"Like you." Not a question, not even a statement, but a glimmer of hope.

"Yes, like me. Like Dad. Like Seth. Like Willy and Patsy. Like your landlord. Lots of people care for you, Jed. In fact, my mother thinks you're pretty terrific, a compliment she rarely applies to any man."

He let out a breath that sounded as if it had been trapped for years. Turning around, he propped one shoulder against the wall. "Your mother, huh? I've never had much luck with mothers."

Keely swallowed, not sure she wanted to continue this, and yet very sure she should. She laced her fingers together, counting the beats of silence, hating the idea of making him feel awkward.

Softly, as if he sensed her strain, he asked, "What do you want to know?"

"It's a long list," she said, depending on her small smile not to scare him away.

To her vast relief, he grinned back. "No doubt."

"You'll answer all my questions?"

"You'll miss the ferry."

"Oh." Keely glanced at her watch. Damn! Twenty minutes was all she had. "You could have agreed to this when I had a lot of time."

"And when would that have been?" he asked with an arch of one eyebrow. "You're either in here slaving over the paperwork or teaching or making sure Irma has made enough food or counseling the kids. The only time you're free is at night. And the potential in that isn't something either of us wants to explore.''

If she hadn't known better she'd have thought he was complaining of neglect. Was he? A memory of Paul floated into her mind, as well as her views on men liking attention. Jed's comments—she didn't want to quite call them complaints—sounded as if her inattention annoyed him.

Since she didn't have time for all her questions, she debated with herself which one she wanted to know the answer to the most.

His relationship with Marcie would be logical, since he'd asked about Paul. Or why he kept a scrapbook. That fascinated her, along with the tiny carved tiger she'd seen in his apartment. She knew he'd saved some of the scrap lumber from the generator's house, and she'd concluded he intended to use it for making toys. But as important as those questions were, a statement Seth had made dwarfed them all.

''Did you ever kill anyone?''

Jed regarded her with such intensity that Keely wished she'd stuck to her original idea and asked about Marcie.

''Yes.''

Nothing more. No explanation. No defense.

''Want to call Seth in here and tie me up until the ferry comes?'' he asked with an unconcerned blandness.

She ignored his sarcasm. ''Tell me about it.''

Again his eyes bored into her. She could read his thoughts. Are you for real? Do you really care or is this just pity in disguise? What will you think when you know? And the most poignant—will you believe me?

"It happened over a woman named Sadie." He paused, and she knew he was expecting her to make a comment like "Isn't it always?" Or "What else is new?"

She stood up, straightening her skirt, more to relieve the dampness in her palms than to smooth out any wrinkles. She pushed aside some papers and perched on the edge of the desk, bringing herself closer to him.

Folding her hands in her lap to stop them from reaching out in any kind of touching gesture, she said, "Jed, I'm not a judge, a jury or even a curiosity seeker. If you don't want to tell me, it's all right."

His gray eyes narrowed, but she saw the fury in them. Not common anger, but a deeply felt rage that made her see suddenly that Jed Corey could kill if he had to.

In a monotone voice, he began. "The bastard had a knife and he'd been doing some drug. LSD was the drug of choice at the time. Sadie was sitting at the table doing her accounts, trying to stretch what she had to pay the month's bills with. I was clearing off some eating tables for her when the guy asked her where the money was."

Jed talked with an almost cold neutrality as if that would make the story easier to tell. His cheeks appeared more hollow, and he shivered once despite the stuffy air in the room.

Keely had questions. Who was Sadie? Where did this happen? How old was Jed? She wisely waited.

"I stood there, scared—God, was I scared—while this spaced-out bastard waved a knife at Sadie. She didn't move, and if I hadn't known her so well I would have thought she faced guys with knives pointed at her throat every day. There were a couple of others in the room, and they beat it to the kitchen like their butts had been burned.''

Keely's thoughts staggered at hearing something she wasn't sure she wanted to listen to. ''You tried to help Sadie?''

''She was all I had,'' he said with such quiet, intense emotion that Keely felt a ruthless hatred for the knife-wielding intruder. ''The only woman who ever gave a damn about me. Yeah, I wanted to gut him. I grabbed a fistful of dirty forks and went at him.'' He stopped to breathe to release the tension. ''Except he got me first.''

Her questions about the scar were answered before he lifted his T-shirt.

Without second thoughts, she ran her fingers across the long scar. The years had faded the mark, but not the feelings behind it. It felt puckery in contrast to the soft hair and smooth skin of his belly.

She allowed her fingers to linger. ''You could have died.''

''The guy thought he'd killed me.'' His laugh was dry and without humor. ''Sadie was all over him. Screaming and swearing. Then he dropped the knife....''

''You got the knife.'' His shirt had settled over her fingers in a bunch, and she slowly withdrew her hand.

''He had his thumbs on the pulse of her throat, squeezing, squeezing. God, she turned red, then white, her eyes rolled back, and I knew if I didn't stop him he'd kill her. I went after him, trying to get him to let go of her. The knife in his belly finally convinced him.''

He hadn't just coldly killed someone, he'd defended and saved someone who couldn't defend herself. ''And Sadie?''

"I don't know. I was in the hospital for a while. By the time I went back to find her she was gone. I looked for her, asked everyone who might have known where she went. Someone told me she went back to New York. I guess she had family there. A year or so later, I heard she died in a Brooklyn shelter." A mixture of cynicism and anger braced his next words. "So much for family."

"Did you love her?"

"I felt more for her than I've ever felt for any woman. Love?" He shrugged. "I don't know anything about that."

She wanted to say there was still time to learn, still time to trust someone again, still time to allow a woman into his life. A memory of the kiss in her cabin suddenly appeared in her thoughts, and with it the faulty idea that she could be that woman.

She changed the focus of the conversation. "They didn't send you to jail or anything, did they? I mean it sounds like you killed that guy not only in self-defense, but to save Sadie."

"Your dad was the judge. He let me go. Called me brave for what I'd done. It was weird. When I threatened him with the knife here in this office, he called me a coward." He looked away as though remembering, then cleared his throat. "Anyway, if I'd been sent up, it wouldn't have been jail. I'd have gone to the training school."

Keely blinked. "But that's for juveniles! How old were you?"

"Fourteen."

"Oh, Jed," she whispered on an unsteady breath. "Sadie...she wasn't...wasn't a girlfriend, was she? She was like a mother to you?"

"Yeah, I guess. She must have been in her forties. She was a volunteer at the shelter where I lived. She took care of the money and anything else that needed doing. Nothing ever shocked her. She taught me how to sew patches on my jeans, and a couple of times when I was drunk she snuck me into her room and let me sleep on a cot she had." He grinned at some fond memory.

"Tell me," she urged.

"Nothing. Just that she was one special lady." He lifted her wrist and checked her watch. "You'll miss the ferry."

She reached up and cupped his cheek. He allowed the touch and then gently lifted her hand away.

"You'll get dirty."

She wanted to kiss him, to hold him, to take away all the awful memories.

He scowled as though he read her mind. "Don't pity me, Keely. I don't want it and I don't like it."

"It isn't pity. It's caring. Caring about a fourteen-year-old boy who killed someone to save the only woman he ever loved. I find that commendable."

"It sounds like some melodramatic soap opera."

"Don't be so afraid of letting the emotion out."

"Oh, I let it out all right. Right into that bastard's gut."

"I don't mean that. That was a reaction to a life-threatening situation. I mean the feelings behind why. Why you didn't run to the kitchen like the others. Why you stayed and protected Sadie."

He said nothing, stalking to the door, the control cloaking any answer she hoped to get.

"Jed."

"Save the counseling for the kids, Keely." He pushed open the screen door and walked out.

She watched from the window as he moved across the grounds. Trying to read his thoughts from his body movements was nearly impossible. Revealing himself took an enormous amount of effort, whereas most people in her experience had difficulty hiding themselves effectively.

Yet, if she thought carefully, he had left some strong clues as to the kind of man he was.

The scrapbook came immediately to mind. Her intent when she went to his apartment had been to get him to come to the Island rather than to pry into his background. She would never have picked up the scrapbook if it hadn't struck her as so unusual. She'd glanced through it without really studying what was there.

She'd seen the picture of the woman with graying hair, eyes that were as lifeless as a mannequin's. Yet despite the dullness and the ragged grimness around her mouth, Keely had seen a stubborn will that seemed to say, I won't give up.

Turk's mother, in the letter she wrote and that Keely read the night before she came to the Island, had expressed that same thought. I won't give up.

She had assumed the scrapbook picture was of Jed's mother, but she guessed now it was Sadie. And after she'd heard his defense of her, she knew why Sadie meant so much to him, why Sadie deserved a place in the treasured scrapbook.

As she watched Jed disappear down the path toward his tent, a new reality swept through her. Dazzling, yes, but also profoundly humbling.

She, too, had her picture in his treasured scrapbook.

The far-reaching implications of being in Jed's scrapbook stayed with Keely for the ferry and taxi ride into Providence. Impossible implications, she concluded as she stepped out of the cab, and gave the driver a generous tip.

"Wow," he said, fisting the twenty. "When did the state get so generous?"

"The traffic was horrendous, Al. You did an outstanding job of not getting us stopped."

"Yeah?" He beamed at the compliment. "I'm gonna get a coffee and doughnuts. When you want me back here?"

Keely glanced at her watch. "Say forty-five minutes?"

"I'll be here. Want I should bring you a Bavarian cream?"

"I'd love one, but I better not. They're a little heavy in this hot weather. See you in a little while."

Half an hour later Keely was sitting in a leather side chair in Judge Robert Nelson's air-conditioned oak-paneled chambers. Idly noting his shelf of golf trophies and the steady ticking of an antique mantel clock, she found her mind strayed to Jed while Judge Nelson read the preliminary reports.

While she sipped coffee laced with heavy cream from a delicate china cup, she thought of Jed at the breakfast table, surrounded by rowdy tough-talking boys and drinking a mug of black coffee with too much sugar. Three heaping teaspoons, to be exact. Never had she known a man who drank coffee so sweet.

The sugar in his coffee was a minor detail not worth a second thought. Yet, with Jed she found herself thinking about it as though it carried some significance. Like the scrapbook. And that certainly was *not* a minor detail.

He was complex and disturbing, she thought. The harder he tried to keep those complexities to himself, the more she wanted to know about him, the more she found herself unable to not think about him.

"Commendable, Keely, commendable," Judge Nelson said, nodding as he read the last report. Finally he laid the folder on his desk, and settled back in his chair. His white golf shirt peeked out from under his judicial robes. At fifty, he had a forehead with permanent furrows, and his hairline was marching away from his face as though intent on escaping the arrival of wrinkles.

It was his smile that charmed and intrigued Keely. It softened his stern features when he chose to use it. As he did now.

"Very commendable," he added.

"I'm glad you approve."

"Preliminary approval. The board will have to study your reports and make a conclusion. I think, however, you aren't in any danger of losing the directorship for at least a week."

"How encouraging."

"You know how the system works. The board is a necessary evil. It's accountable to the state to make sure the Island does what the taxpayers are paying for."

"So I continue to write reports."

"Sorry. Also, we'll be visiting the Island. I don't know when. The visit is supposed to be unannounced."

Keely leaned forward and put her cup down. "I can hardly wait," she said, trying to calculate the board's idea of unannounced. Would they arrive at three in the morning?

"What about Corey? You barely mention him in these," he said, tapping the folder with a pen.

"Was I supposed to report on Jed?"

"I would have liked a little more detail than you have here. You're usually not so vague."

The vagueness, she realized, came from a fear that if she got into the subject of Jed she'd reveal more than she wanted to. "There isn't a lot to tell. He does what he's there for."

Judge Nelson regarded her with one of his looks reserved for a bail jumper. Keely crossed her legs and gave him her best counseling look.

The judge grinned. "You look like you're getting ready to ask me why I beat my wife. Okay, Keely, I'll settle for Corey does his job. I guess that's what I really wanted to know."

"How's Eunice?"

"Enjoying our new granddaughter. I may have to get a second job to pay for the baby gifts. I think she's depleted three baby shops and starting on her fourth."

Keely laughed. "Sounds wonderful."

"In fact, Rosemary has been spending a lot of time with Eunice. I think she's a little envious."

Keely stood up. "She's been lonely since Dad died."

"I know, but she's also ready to be a grandmother."

"How did we get on this subject?"

"Keely, you know how I felt about Edgar. He was one of the finest judges the state ever had and a good friend, but he's gone. As far as the Island goes, it was a good effort on his part, but frankly, I can't see you living out your life over there."

"Ah," she said, with enough bite to let him know she didn't agree with his opinion. "And your personally handed-down decision for my happiness is giving my mother grandchildren?"

"Am I about to get a lecture on feminism?" he asked with too much humor in his voice.

"I wouldn't dream of lecturing you on how to line up your golf trophies, never mind anything as volatile as feminism."

"It's ruining the family unit in this country."

"You don't really believe that." When he placed his hands behind his head and simply looked at her, she felt a sickening lurch as if the cream in her coffee had curdled in her stomach. "Yes, I guess you do. Of course, the drugs pouring across our borders, the guns anyone can buy with just a driver's license, a justice system that winks at rapists—none of those things are hurting the country. Only feminism."

"I should know better than to argue with you." He held both hands up to signal he didn't want to debate with her. "All right. I'll allow that feminism isn't entirely to blame."

"If I didn't like you so much, I'd tell you to take your opinions and—"

"Uh-uh, Keely. I could find you in contempt."

She lifted an eyebrow, recognizing his threat was as meaningless as when she was six and left bubble gum on his gavel. Then he'd threatened her with life without any possibility of parole.

He smiled. "I'm wearing my robes, you know."

"You mean you're hiding your golf shirt."

"Poor Jed Corey. How does he deal with you?"

She slung her purse over her shoulder. "I'll send the next set of reports if that's all right."

"Fine. You didn't answer my question."

"Call it my feminist right. Give my love to Eunice, and a welcome-to-the-world hug for your new granddaughter."

He rose from behind his desk and crossed the room as she opened the door. "How about letting me give you a keep-up-the-good-work hug?"

His eyes were warm and guileless, and she welcomed the hug of support.

Outside, she found Al and his cab, double-parked in a restricted zone, waiting for her. A meter maid stood by the driver's side, chatting.

"Okay, Al, now I know the secret," Keely said as she settled inside. Al maneuvered the cab through a few precarious turns to the entrance ramp to I-95. "You charm all the meter maids, and then they don't ticket you, right?"

"I buy them doughnuts."

"I should have known. Bribery."

"Hey, what goes around comes around." He caught her gaze in the rearview mirror. "I meant to ask you on the trip here, but with the son of a—oops, sorry, the confounded traffic, I forgot. I hear Jed Corey is on that Island with you."

Keely sighed. There was no escape from Jed even on a clogged interstate. "Jed is there."

"How's he treat you?"

Strange question, she thought. "Jed treats me fine. Why?"

"He used to live with a woman. Forgot her name. Uh, Mary or something."

"Marcie?"

"You know her?"

"I've heard the name."

Al nodded. "Anyway, heard tell he threw her out. She was crazy about the guy. I mean she did everything for him. Washed his clothes. Cooked for him. Heard tell she was a real firecracker in the bedroom. And he dumped her.''

Discussing Jed's personal life as if it were back-fence gossip didn't appeal to Keely. Although she knew nothing about his relationship with Marcie, if Jed had dumped her as Al said, Keely knew there was another side to the story. ''Maybe he had good reason,'' she said demurely.

Al floored the gas pedal to get around a bus. ''She wanted to marry him. I mean, she gave the guy everything, and she asks one thing and he tosses her.''

Keely put her head back and closed her eyes. The Jed Corey Al talked about was not the Jed Corey she knew. Or maybe it was. She couldn't imagine him ever considering anything as emotionally binding as marriage. Paul would have loved a woman like Marcie. All that domesticity was what he liked.

Yet Jed could have had it forever and refused it.

So what did prompt the breakup with Marcie? she wondered. Fear of marriage or commitment? Or something even deeper? Fear of love? Perhaps he didn't know what it was, but then he might also know what it wasn't.

She felt the headache begin when Al pulled into the Aquidneck Dock parking lot.

Barbara Isherwood stood a few yards away, wearing a caramel-colored linen suit and a lemon-ice cotton sweater, yellow sandals and carrying a Nantucket Lightship basket. Around her neck trailed a scarf long enough to stretch from Newport to the Island.

Beside her, straining against the fingers locked on her slender arm was a rumpled, sullen teenager.

Chapter 7

Barbara, it's been a long time," Keely said, not about to be hypocritical and say she was ecstatic to see her. The girl beside Barbara lowered her head even more, pressing her chin into her clavicle.

Offering no return greeting, Barbara tossed her head and swept her hand in the general direction of the Island. "Finally we can talk."

Keely's interest centered on the teenager. She wondered what the girl would do if Barbara released her. Would she run? And who was she?

Keely guessed her to be about fourteen. Her shoulder-length wheat-blond hair frizzed around her face in a beguiling way, although Keely was sure the tense teenager rarely thought of herself as beguiling. In a high school crowd, with her stiff-postured rebelliousness, she would have blended unnoticed. Yet here, bolted to Barbara, Keely picked up an impression of desperate embarrassment.

To Barbara, she said, "We can save each other a lot of time. I'm not interested in selling the beach house."

Barbara shook her head and plucked her scarf off her face where the bay breeze was determined to put it. "No. No, not the beach house. I wanted to see you about something else." She consulted a thin gold wristwatch. "I don't have a lot of time," she murmured and glanced toward the entrance of the parking lot with an eager expectation that contrasted sharply with her impatience with the teenager. "My plane leaves from Logan later tonight, and I want to get this settled."

Still, she'd said nothing about the girl, who had managed to put a few inches between herself and Barbara. The real estate agent moved slightly, flexing her fingers around the girl's flesh.

Jewelry clanked when the teenager moved. Keely found herself fascinated with her earrings—a garish dangle of silver coils and colored beads that almost reached her slumped shoulders. She also had on the teenage accoutrements of label-acceptable clothes, plus a pouty mouth and a self-consciousness she was trying very hard to hide.

Since Barbara didn't seem inclined to identify the girl, Keely said, "Hi, I'm Keely Lockwood. I love your earrings. Where did you get them?"

The teenager appeared startled to be addressed, and chewed on her lip.

Barbara gave her arm a shake. "Answer her. I swear, the rudeness of kids today is appalling. Don't you agree, Keely?"

The girl cringed, and Keely wanted to shake Barbara. "It's never rude to think first about what you're going to say."

The teenager's eyes, blue as bachelor's buttons and with lashes laden with mascara, opened wide, showing defiance fringed with shyness. She held Keely's gaze long enough for Keely to sneak in a smile.

"April, you're not making a good impression," Barbara said, while at the same time trying to get April's wrinkled shirt collar to either lie down or stand up. April tried to pull away. Her eyes snapped with hostility, her mouth set in a long practiced pout.

Immune, Barbara breezed on. "I'm at my wit's end. She has everything—clothes, jewelry, money—and does she appreciate it? Of course not. You'd think after I've worked so hard to give her things, the least she could do is cooperate. Now, I ask you? Is that too much to expect? I hope you can do something with her."

Keely stepped aside to allow two men carrying a heavy wooden crate to pass.

"Wait a minute, Barbara. We seem to be on some odd wavelengths. What are you talking about?"

Barbara rolled her eyes as though Keely, too, were as ignorant and unappreciative of her sacrifice as April. Barbara gave the girl another shake. "For goodness sake, April, try not to look so pained. You act like I'm sending you to Siberia." To Keely, she said, "April's my daughter."

Her daughter! Of course, Keely thought, somewhat stunned she hadn't immediately made that assumption—perhaps because the few times Barbara ever talked about anything personal, it involved some man she was seeing, or some real estate sale in which she'd made an astronomical amount of money. Not once could Keely recall Barbara's ever mentioning a daughter. The resemblance was there, although April didn't and probably never would have her mother's lush fullness.

For the first time she spoke. "I won't stay." Keely wasn't surprised at the combativeness in the teenager's eyes.

"And where do you think you're going to go, Miss Priss? You failed swimming lessons, so we can eliminate that. Don't stick your chin out at me. Since running away is what you do best, then the Island is perfect."

"I'll find a way. Maybe I'll kill myself."

Keely felt a suffocating coldness at the threat.

Barbara eyed her daughter as though the idea was preposterous. "Oh, God, don't be so melodramatic."

April's lips thinned so that they almost disappeared.

"Anyway, Keely," Barbara said, "it isn't like you'll have to put up with her for long. Just a little more than two weeks. I'll be in Chicago for a few days, and then I'm finally going to take the vacation I've put off for three years. Two weeks in Hawaii. And do I need it."

Keely watched April's lips move, and in the tiniest of voices she heard the words "I hate you."

She searched around for some way to say no to Barbara, but at the same time not make April feel rejected. Barbara's cold "it isn't like you'll have to put up with her for long" fueled both her reaction as a counselor and her human instinct to pull April away from the woman. "Barbara, excuse us just a minute."

Barbara let go of the teenager, and April leaped away as if she'd escaped from prison. Keely didn't touch her, but urged her out of her mother's earshot.

"I hate her, I hate her," the girl cried, and there was no mistaking the seriousness of her tone. It went beyond a teenager's annoyance at authority. April swiped at eyes that had obviously cried too many times. Tracks of sticky mascara dirtied her cheeks.

Keely would have liked to draw her into her arms and comfort her, but she sensed April wouldn't go for that.

Then April's words came tumbling out as though they'd been building for years. "She's always yelling about something. And she acts like it's a big deal when she doesn't. Yell, I mean. Like I'm supposed to be grateful when she talks in a normal voice."

Keely didn't try to defend Barbara's actions. "April, what did she tell you about the Island?"

The rebellion swelled through her answer. "That it's gonna straighten me out. You know what I say to that?" Then she swore, the profanity explicit and delivered like a seasoned veteran. "She doesn't care what happens to me. I bet she wishes I'd never been born. All she cares about is her vacation. I know she's going with that scumbag she's been sleeping with. She tries to lie about it and tell me they're just friends." She shuddered in disgust. "Does she think I'm that dumb?"

Keely thought of Tommy, the boy on the Island with the potato peeler, who'd justified having it by claiming he loved carrots. She, too, had been annoyed that Tommy considered her stupid.

Perhaps in Barbara's situation the pretense was an attempt to keep her mother image intact. At least she'd showed some concern about what her daughter thought. The other possibility was more disturbing. Did Barbara view April's noncommunication as a sign of obliviousness to her own actions?

"Isn't there someone you can stay with while she's gone?" Keely asked.

"No."

"No one? Not even a friend?"

Look what we've got for you:

… A FREE 20k gold electroplate chain
… plus a sampler set of 4 terrific Silhouette Intimate Moments® novels, specially selected by our editors.

… PLUS a surprise mystery gift that will delight you.

All this just for trying our Reader Service!

If you wish to continue in the Reader Service, you'll get 4 new Silhouette Intimate Moments® novels every month—before they're available in stores. That's SNEAK PREVIEWS for just $2.74★ per book—21¢ less than the cover price—and FREE home delivery besides!

Plus There's More!

With your monthly book shipments, you'll also get our newsletter, packed with news of your favorite authors and upcoming books—FREE! And as a valued reader, we'll be sending you additional free gifts from time to time— as a token of our appreciation for being a home subscriber.

THERE IS NO CATCH. You're not required to buy a single book, ever. You may cancel Reader Service privileges anytime, if you want. All you have to do is write "cancel" on your statement or simply return your shipment of books to us at our cost. The free gifts are yours anyway. It's a super-sweet deal if ever there was one. Try us and see!

Get 4 FREE full-length Silhouette Intimate Moments® novels.

Plus

this lovely 20k gold electroplate chain

Plus

a surprise free gift

▼ PLUS LOTS MORE! MAIL THIS CARD TODAY ▼

Silhouette's Best-Ever "Get Acquainted" Offer

PLACE STICKER FOR 6 FREE GIFTS HERE

Yes, I'll try Silhouette books under the terms outlined on the opposite page. Send me 4 free Silhouette Intimate Moments® novels, a free electroplated gold chain and a free mystery gift.

240 CIS YAEU (U-S-IM-03/90)

NAME _____

ADDRESS _____ APT. _____

CITY _____

STATE _____ ZIP CODE _____

PRINTED IN U.S.A.

Don't forget...

... Return this card today and receive 4 free books, free electroplated gold chain and free mystery gift.

... You will receive books before they're available in stores.

... No obligation to buy. You can cancel at any time by writing "cancel" on your statement or returning a shipment to us at our cost.

If offer card is missing, write to: Silhouette Books®
901 Fuhrmann Blvd., P.O. Box 1867, Buffalo, N.Y. 14269-1867

BUSINESS REPLY CARD

First Class   Permit No. 717   Buffalo, NY

Postage will be paid by addressee

Silhouette® Books
901 Fuhrmann Blvd.
P.O. Box 1867
Buffalo, NY 14240-9952

No Postage
Necessary
If Mailed
In The
United States

"I'm not a baby," April said. "She treats me like I'm two years old. She can't make me do anything. I'll do what I want."

Keely stopped herself from commenting that the do-as-I-want mentality wasn't very adult. But then April had a good teacher of immature attitudes. Barbara was bent on doing what *she* wanted, and she apparently viewed April as more of an interference than a concern.

"I know this won't upset you, but the Island isn't for girls. Only boys."

The teenager's answer surprised Keely, who had expected her to be relieved.

"I don't like boys and they don't like me. I got zits and I couldn't win last place in a wet T-shirt contest." She folded her arms across her breasts, which Keely had to admit were small, but April's image problems went deeper than her bra size.

Barbara sailed over to them, her scarf flying out behind her.

"I hope you have the details all worked out. I have to run. April's suitcase and her backpack are over there to be put on the ferry."

She offered her cheek to her daughter; April backed away from it.

Keely grabbed Barbara's arm before she sailed off again. "Wait a minute! You can't just run off and leave April here as though—" A quick glance at April told Keely not to finish the sentence. She shifted subjects. "Where did you get the idea the Island took girls?"

"From your father."

If Barbara had told her the Easter Bunny, she wouldn't have been more stunned.

"Dad? He never had young girls there. He wouldn't even allow me there when I was growing up."

"He told me that when I called him last year, when April tried to run away for the third time. He also told me he was in the process of working out an arrangement with the state so that he could take girls. It had something to do with there being no women on the Island to deal with girls' problems."

"And there still aren't. We're simply not equipped for girls, in terms of privacy or staff."

"But you're there."

"I'm the director. It's true, I do the counseling, but other than Irma, our cook, there aren't any women. Look, Barbara, if you want my opinion, April needs more than to be shunted away while you go off on vacation."

"I've waited three years for this vacation. My plans are made. Anyway, she and I don't get along very well. A separation would probably do us both good."

Keely lowered her head and mouthed a swearword. If she'd ever seen a classic case of self-pity and selfishness, Barbara Isherwood was it.

She thought of her options. Make a phone call and see if she could find someone to take April. Tell Barbara her first responsibility was to her daughter, although from the sneer on April's face and the stubbornness on Barbara's, she held little hope that that would do any good. If Dad were alive what would he do? she asked herself.

Instinctively, she knew he wouldn't have walked away from a girl who needed help. If he'd told Barbara he wanted to include girls in the program, then eventually he would have done it. Her father had never turned his back on a kid in trouble, and Keely didn't intend to turn her back on April.

Certainly, it could work. Seth had that roll-away bed in his room, which was originally for Jed. It could be moved into Keely's cabin.

And her father's dream. What better way to fulfill it than to begin a new venture that he hadn't lived long enough to start?

"April, if you don't mind sharing a cabin with me—"

"Of course she doesn't mind," Barbara answered in a breezy, it's-all-settled manner. "Try to behave yourself, April. Ms. Lockwood is going to a lot of trouble for you."

April swallowed. Keely had the strongest urge to slap Barbara Isherwood across the face.

A red sports car pulled into the parking area. Barbara brightened and grinned almost girlishly. "That's Bruce." She breathed his name as if it were a synonym for perfection. "I have to run."

Bruce didn't emerge from the car, but Keely heard April murmur, "Scumbag." He did, however, honk. Two short impatient honks.

Barbara fiddled with her hair, swept her scarf back, gave April a kiss that landed in the air above her cheek, took a deep breath and sucked in her cheeks. "Bruce doesn't like to wait," she said, clearly implying something more intimate than horn-honking impatience.

When she opened the car door and climbed inside, Keely saw the man's hand slide languorously up Barbara's thigh. Waiting did seem to bother Bruce, Keely thought, feeling a pang of envy. Her mind skittered back to the Island. To her cabin, to the bees and to the hot lick of fire Jed had left on her mouth.

Pushing aside her warm thoughts about Jed, she and
April walked over to the ferry slip. April hoisted the
backpack over her shoulder and lifted the suitcase.
Keely motioned April to precede her onto the ferry, then
okayed a load of food that Irma had ordered.

While the bay churned beneath them and the sea gulls
circled, Keely and April stood at the railing, watching
the shore recede.

"He's younger than her," April offered curtly. "I
think it's disgusting."

"April, some men like older women."

"You oughta see them. They act like they're over-
sexed. I came home from school one day and they were
making out in the kitchen."

Making out, Keely thought, her mind once again
settling on Jed. "April..."

"You know what she told me later? She does think
I'm dumb. She said they were just kissing. Kissing!"

Keely thought Barbara's denial as well as her timing
were rather pathetic, but in an obscure way there was
something good in the denial—Barbara's knowing that
her impulsive actions could have a disturbing effect on
April. "In defense of your mother," Keely began, but
April cut her off.

"Defense! She was... Forget it. You'd probably slap
my face if I said it."

"I would never slap your face. And I do know what
she was doing. But just because she's your mother
doesn't mean she isn't a woman who—" how could she
put this clinically? "—who enjoys the company of a
man." Terrific, she thought; she sounded like some
prude who'd just found out sex meant more than a
word for the male and female genders.

April eyed her suspiciously.

Keely began again. "I think she might want to keep her image intact for you."

"Yeah, right. If she cares so much about me, then why doesn't she say so instead of telling me Bruce is her friend?"

"Because mothers like to believe their children are more innocent than they usually are. What do you think of Bruce?"

"I told you."

"How does he treat you?"

She shrugged. "Okay, I guess."

"For a scumbag?"

April smiled for the first time. Not exactly a school's-out-for-the-summer smile, but it was an encouraging start.

The Island got larger as the ferry chugged closer. Keely could see some of the kids scattered near the dock. She automatically searched for Jed.

"Am I gonna have to do what the boys do?" April asked when the ferry began the final turn toward the Island.

"At the moment they're in the process of building a house for the new generator. Jed will show you the ropes, or I could use some help in the office, if you'd like to start there."

"Is Jed one of the boys?"

"No. He works for me." Keely suddenly realized how anxious she was to see him.

After the ferry maneuvered into the wooden slip, Keely squinted at the kids working on the dock. She was also trying to find Jed.

Turk and Snakeman were busy stacking lobster pots. The other kids were scattered around doing various tasks, including a rather creative paint job on the rowboat Jed had repaired.

All of them came to a stunned halt when they saw April.

Turk made no attempt to hide his interest. "Hey! Check it out, will ya! Man, is she for real?"

Keely stepped off the ferry, scanning the trees and the paths. "Turk, where's Jed?"

"Doin' the bees." He elbowed Snakeman. "Hey, man, it wiggles and who cares if it walks and talks?"

Keely stalked over to Turk and took his arm, forcefully turning him around, so he couldn't ogle April.

"Hey, you're breakin' my arm."

"Cut the swagger, Turk. I thought you were going to do the bees."

"Yeah, well, I did. Jed told me to get a stick and a burlap bag."

"For what? He isn't trying to catch a snake."

"I didn't hang around. Man, those things sting, you know."

"So you left Jed to get stung. He hates bees."

Turk peered at her as if she'd turned into a raving idiot. "Jeez, if I'd known you were gonna blow your jets, I'd have stayed with Jed."

Keely closed her mouth and took a quick breath. So Jed wasn't there to meet her. It wasn't as if he was supposed to, yet she couldn't rid herself of the crushing disappointment.

A disappointment she hadn't been aware of until she stepped off the ferry and didn't see him. What a great example she was setting for April, she thought in disgust. She wasn't much better than Barbara—more interested in a man than in her responsibility.

April stood at the ferry railing as if stepping out to the dock was hazardous.

"Who's the dynamite-looking chick?" Turk asked, jamming his hands in his pockets. His eyes narrowed when he faced Snakeman, an obvious attempt, Keely decided, to establish rights and draw proprietary lines.

She glared at him with a no-way look.

He smiled winningly with the kind of charm that Keely knew was at least ninety percent proof when he used it. "Okay, okay. Jeez. Don't freak out. Who is she?"

Keely took four deep breaths solely for the purpose of not coming back with another sharp answer. "Her name is April. She's a friend of mine, and she's going to be here for a few days."

"April, huh? Where's May and June?" The clichéd comment brought a round of raucous laughter that Turk encouraged enthusiastically.

"Turk, try to enjoy your own humor," she said dryly while urging a skittish April off the ferry. "It wouldn't hurt any of you to ease off the jungle and street mentality."

April hovered by Keely's back like a child hiding behind a door.

Keely counted the empty lobster pots. "How many lobsters were in the pots?"

Turk told her and then said Irma was cooking them for dinner. He kept looking at April, who blushed, shifted her feet and finally, out of desperation, clutched her backpack to her chest.

Keely said, "One of you guys can get her suitcase. It goes in my cabin."

They all moved with more speed than Keely had seen since they'd arrived on the Island. Turk led the way, and when a fight broke out as to who was going to carry the suitcase, Jed came stalking toward them.

"What's going on?" he growled, walking from the dirt path onto the dock.

He glanced first at the boys, then drew his brows into a who-are-you frown at April. When his gaze settled on Keely, his gray eyes were all smoke and silver. She swore she also saw the tiniest amount of possessiveness. A sizzling sensation inside her weakened her knees.

Keely swallowed. He'd removed his shirt, and was carrying it bunched in his fist as if he'd grabbed it on the run. Sleek, sweaty, muscled, his chest was a fantasy for her fingers. Her eyes drank him in as though he belonged to her, as though their relationship were intimate and not professional. As though she had the right to think erotic thoughts while she waited for him to sweep her up into a long deep kiss.

She spotted the two swollen places on his back, and covered them with her fingers. Instantly she was aware that she felt compelled to touch him, to connect with him in any way possible. His skin felt hot and damp.

"Ouch!" He stiffened away from her. "Hell! What are you doing?"

She dropped her hand, her palm still holding his warmth. "You got stung."

"Yeah." He pulled on his shirt, then raked back his hair. "They didn't care much for the stick or the burlap."

She dragged her thoughts back to the subject instead of the sensual path they were headed. "You got rid of the hive?"

"I got rid of it." He kept looking at April as if she were a mirage. He turned to Keely, took her arm and pulled her away from the others. Far enough away so they wouldn't be overheard.

"Who is she?" Jed asked, staring down at her. A trickle of sweat inched down his temple.

Keely felt just a little dizzy. "You should put ointment on your back. I have some stuff in my cabin. I could—"

"Rub it on me?" He scowled, his eyes suspicious and dangerous.

"They're in an awkward spot for you to get at. It would just take a minute."

"I'll live from the bee stings. Your rubbing anything on me would cause a worse problem." He planted one hand low on his hip and jerked his thumb over his shoulder in the direction of April. "Who's the girl?"

Keely clamped a death hold on her wayward thoughts and cleared her throat. "Her name is April Isherwood. She's going to be with us for a few weeks."

He looked at her as though she'd said April had been beamed down from Mars. "You're not serious."

She met his eyes. "Very serious."

"Send her back where she came from." He turned around, and with his thumb and forefinger, he whistled. The shrill sound traveled through the late-afternoon breeze. Responding to his command, every boy dropped what he was carrying and came to attention like a row of fresh recruits. April, who'd bent down to examine one of the lobster pots, looked as though she wanted to crawl into one.

The ferry captain appeared on the deck and lifted his head to indicate he'd heard the whistle. Jed strode back down to the dock and stopped in front of April.

"Sweetheart," he said gently, "the ferry will take you back to the mainland."

April stared up at him, her mouth slightly open, her eyes wide with awe. After three gulps, she managed a "But Keely said—"

"I know, but with the boys here, it just won't work."

Keely marched over. "Now wait just a minute. April, you're staying." The boys gave a roar of approval that she ignored. "Might I remind you, Jed, that I'm the director here. I make the decisions on who stays and who goes."

He stood perfectly still, his eyes boring into her. The tension rolled between them like a suffocating heat.

Finally, without swearing, without breathing any harder than normal, he turned away from her. He waved the ferry off and told the boys to move their butts. Keely touched him as he passed by her without a glance. "Everything will work out. I know what I'm doing," she whispered.

She might as well have been invisible. He kept walking, his boots moving across the rugged terrain as though there were no rocks, no holes, nothing to trip him up.

Annoyed, Keely wished a bee would appear and sting him again. Damn him! Why couldn't he just yell and get angry? Or at least realize that this was her problem, since she was the director?

April whispered behind her. "Wow! Oh, wow. He's gorgeous. Hot and kinda wild and . . . wow!"

"I thought you didn't like boys," Keely snapped.

"Are you kidding?" She practically swooned. "If you think he's a boy . . . wow!"

"He's off-limits, April. And besides, he's too old for you."

"I wonder if he's ever modeled jeans. I mean, jeez, I could just stand around and watch him walk in jeans. And buttoned ones!"

Keely rolled her eyes and started up the path.

April skipped along beside Keely. The girl's animation over Jed brought back the headache that had begun when she saw Barbara on the dock.

April giggled. "I bet he knows how to kiss and make your toes sizzle, huh?"

She danced in front of Keely, skipping backward, her blue eyes a blend of mischief and rapture. Amazing, Keely thought, annoyed that the teenager's transformation had come about because of the way a pair of jeans hung on Jed Corey's hips.

"April, I think we'd better get a few things clear about the rules here on the Island." Keely listed the rules, including the one about no sex.

April's expression changed, and Keely wasn't sure if she was surprised or pleased. "You mean he isn't sleeping with you?"

"No, he is not." She said it too quickly and hoped April didn't read anything into her haste. "The rule applies to everyone."

"Yeah, but what if it didn't? The rule, I mean."

"He's not my type."

"Hey, if I were you, I'd change my taste in men. Wow!"

Changing her taste in men was the thought Keely considered while she got April settled, and during a very long dinner with the boys, who showed off as if they hadn't seen a female their age in years. The rest of the staff welcomed April, although they seemed guarded as to how her stay was going to work out. April bloomed as though never in her life had all the attention been on her. Seth kept looking from Keely to April and back to Keely with a distressed expression. Keely had no trouble reading his thoughts: "I wish your dad was here."

And then there was Jed. He ate but said very little beyond complimenting Irma on her biscuits, and telling the boys that the next day they'd begin the final construction on the house for the generator. He never glanced at Keely.

When the meal was finished, he stood. Keely expected him to walk out and ignore her the way he'd done since the incident on the dock. Instead he waited until everyone had left. Irma hustled Seth through the door into the kitchen, giving Jed and Keely more privacy than Keely wanted.

He was going to kiss her, she was sure of it.

He was going to slowly cross the room, come to a stop in front of her and lift her up to ravage her mouth.

Intuition. Vibes. That tiny seed of possessiveness she'd seen in his eyes that afternoon. She sensed them all.

Her breasts tightened, her bra suddenly too snug against her nipples. She gave in to a dewy lethargy that spread and grew dangerously close to a heavy arousal. She knew if she allowed the kiss, her claim that he wasn't her type would be a flimsy farce.

His gray eyes held her so enthralled, and she felt as though her soul was being revealed.

Anticipation burned inside her.

Then his words emptied into the room. "I want to know why you lied to me."

Chapter 8

The room seemed to shrink around her, sucking up the air.

"What?" She barely managed the single word.

"You heard me," he snapped, confirming for her that the last thing on his mind was kissing her.

The long table separated them, the top damp where Irma had wiped up the food spilled during a squabble over who got to pass the fruit salad to April.

Jed leaned forward, palms flat on the wooden surface. "You left here today to see Nelson and a real estate agent. At least that's the story I got. And you came back with the potential for disaster."

At least he hadn't started this in front of the others, she thought thankfully. Her body felt numb as the last threads of anticipation broke.

On a sigh of annoyance she said, "The potential being April? Really Jed, do you think that's fair?"

"Why didn't you tell me?"

"Tell you what?"

"That April was coming."

"Because I didn't know."

He gave her a steady disbelieving glower.

"I didn't!" She resented his assumption, and at the same time found herself annoyed that she cared a whit what he thought. "Do you want me to tell you what happened, or would you prefer to hold on to your excuse to be angry with me?"

That seemed to jar him. "I don't know what you're talking about."

"What happened to all that control you're so proud of? Since I got back here you've acted like a whole beehive stung you instead of two little bees."

He walked over to a chair, settled himself in it as though he anticipated a long night and wanted to get comfortable. He propped his booted feet on the corner of the table and crossed his ankles. With a heavy sigh, he dragged both hands through his hair. His gaze traveled across the room to her eyes like an arrow aimed at a target.

"My anger will wait. Why is she here?"

Keely stood in spite of her legs' feeling as though they were incapable of supporting her. She had no intention of allowing him to intimidate her, she thought, walking the few steps to where he was sitting. She remained on her feet, relishing the fact that she towered over him. He didn't move.

When her left thigh brushed his knee, she laced her fingers together to keep them still.

In a steady although somewhat raspy voice, she told Jed about the meeting with Barbara Isherwood, and why she'd brought April back to the Island. For a long time he didn't say anything, and Keely wondered if he still thought she was lying.

"A soft spot for hurt creatures," he murmured. His hand captured her laced fingers and drew her forward. Keely didn't pull back or shake off his touch.

"It's called caring, Jed." As she cared for him, she admitted to herself. And she did care about Jed. Perhaps too much, and in ways that had nothing to do with friendship or working together.

The cotton ribbing around the bottom of her white sweater seemed to fascinate him. She hadn't had time to change clothes since her return to the Island, and she still wore the screened-print sweater and pink skirt. Wisps of her hair had escaped the figure-eight chignon, giving her a slightly mussed appearance.

"Do you know what the talk is among the guys?" he asked.

"What?"

"Who's gonna get April? My money is on Turk."

She pushed away his fingers, which were investigating a rose on her sweater. "A typical macho mentality. Since you seem to be privy to the inside dirt, you can deliver a message to them for me. April is off-limits. No touchy-feely and no leering looks. She's staying in my cabin. In fact, she'll be working right in the office with me. The only time she'll see the boys is at meals."

He was silent, as though considering if what she said would work. "Do Nelson and the board know about this?"

In truth, Keely hadn't given any thought to either. While she was aware she was probably breaking some bureaucratic rule, she also knew that April needed help immediately. Then her heart did a little thump. The surprise inspection that Judge Nelson had mentioned.

What was she going to do about that? She couldn't hide
April. Well, of course she wouldn't try to hide her.
Turning her back and leaving a minor, who was a three-
time runaway, standing on Aquidneck Dock would
certainly not have pleased the board.

She swallowed and lifted her chin, feeling stubborn
and even a little defiant. "It's what Dad would have
done. His intention for the future was to include girls
here at the Island. He just didn't live long enough to get
a program for them started."

He gave her another disbelieving look, but this time
his eyes were concerned rather than angry. "They don't
know, do they?"

"No!" she replied, coming close to shouting.

She saw no reason to tell him her information came
by way of Barbara, a fact that, she realized with a bald
clarity, she resented. Not the information, but the messenger.

Why had her father not told her he planned such a
venture? He must have known that she would have
leaped at the opportunity to be involved in his work. It
seemed that even as an adult, she realized bleakly, he
hadn't wanted her on the Island.

She tried to draw her hands away from Jed, but she
might as well have tried to fly. With his hold firm on her
wrist, he lowered his boots to the floor and came up out
of the chair. "Your neck gets blotchy when you're nervous."

"Let me go, Jed."

"Do you know your dream is likely to become a
classic nightmare if she stays? What happens when the
board finds out? You think they're going to ignore her
because you're the Judge's daughter? Like hell. Either
way, babe, your butt is up to here in . . ." He flattened

his hand against the hammering pulse in her neck. "Let's just call it trouble."

"I didn't think about the board! I couldn't leave her, don't you see? Her mother said she'd already run away a number of times."

"And where is her mother?" Jed asked with more rancor and viciousness than the question deserved. She wondered if the depth of his emotion had more to do with his own mother than with April's. "Flying off with her lover sure doesn't sound like mother love and concern."

"I think in her own way Barbara does love April. She thinks material things are the answer, the more the better. April, of course, isn't saying no, but she's crying out for some strong support. Support for her as a person. She's scared, Jed."

Jed drew Keely closer, and in a touch so gentle she thought she'd imagined it, he brushed his mouth across her forehead. "Like I said, a soft spot for hurt creatures."

Wanting to touch him, needing to be held, hoping he wouldn't fight her decision, she shyly slipped her arms around his waist and rested her head against his chest. Strength and support, she thought. April needed it and so did she.

Then remembering their promise to each other, she tried to pull away, but he wouldn't let her go.

She murmured, "We decided we wouldn't touch each other, remember?"

"Yeah."

"This isn't dangerous, is it? This is just two people who work together finding comfort in each other."

His breathing stopped and Keely counted five beats.

"One of those people wanted to rub my back this afternoon," he finally continued.

"Ointment on bee stings is comforting."

"Okay."

She blinked as he set her away from him. Brushing a wisp of hair off her cheek, he asked, "And the ointment is in your cabin, right?"

"Uh, yes. In my cabin."

"And since April is there, it should be safe, shouldn't it?"

She scowled. "If you think I'm going to put stuff on your back in front of April, you're crazy. She thinks you're the hottest-looking thing she's seen since she discovered there are two sexes."

If she'd had any idea he was going to be flattered, she was mistaken. In a scoffing tone, he muttered, "And you thought only the boys had dirty minds."

"You're here to help me. You take care of the boys. I'll handle April. Wait in my office and I'll go get the ointment."

Wait in her office.

It had been one long day of waiting. From the moment she walked onto the ferry that afternoon on her way to see Nelson, Jed had felt as though part of the Island's life and energy had left with her.

He'd thought only about her, to the point where he got careless and almost sliced his hand with the power saw. It was bad enough he had bee stings on his back; a bandaged hand would have made him look like the walking wounded. The whole concept that Keely Lockwood had somehow made that deep an impression on him amazed and disturbed him.

He'd seriously considered leaving the Island for a few days—mostly to clear his head of her. It had to be their constant contact that made her stay in his thoughts long into the night. Other women he'd known barely managed to keep his attention when he was with them.

He knew his feelings were all mixed up with gratitude to her father, and the need to not let anything happen to the Judge's daughter. The fact that the hole in his soul didn't hurt was the one change he couldn't ignore. Keely had had a profound effect on the part of him that no one had ever penetrated. Not Sadie. Not Judge Lockwood.

He prowled the small office, knowing he shouldn't wait for her, while at the same time knowing there was no other place he wanted to be.

The window was open, the night as devoid of light as the dark dangerous thoughts his mind was conjuring up. Since her first suggestion that afternoon of putting ointment on the bee stings, he'd been obsessed with the idea. He told himself it was a valid excuse to feel her hands on him.

Valid or not, bee stings or not, the core of the excuse was her hands. Light, soothing, rubbing. And then what?

More rubbing? A kiss maybe. Her breasts in his hands, heavy and flushed, yet soft and wonderful. Today when he saw her in the sweater, he'd imagined her nipples were the same shade of red as the roses printed on the material. Buds waiting to be brushed and smelled and kissed.

Why the hell was he trying to analyze the feeling? Do it. Take her as far as she allows. What great success would he earn if he never touched her? Besides proving to himself that Jed Corey didn't lose control. If he did touch her, it would become too easy to think that maybe, just maybe, a commitment to Keely Lock-wood . . .

Forget it.

It wasn't that she outclassed him, which she did. It wasn't that she was the Judge's daughter, which she was. It wasn't that she made him so hot that his rea-soning processes smoked and burned until there was nothing but ash.

No, it was none of those. Like the word *love, com-mitment* seemed unreal. If he'd learned anything in the past thirty-six years, it was that there was safety in trusting hard facts. Love and commitment were easy to say, easy to promise, but in reality, they were misty emotions scribbled on Valentine's Day cards and acted out in the movies.

Yeah, he'd missed her today. Missed knowing she was in the office while he and the boys worked.

When he'd walked down the path and seen her on the dock, with the sun in her hair, her skirt and sweater swirling around her, he'd experienced an unexpected joy. He'd also felt a surge of a too familiar arousal, but this time it had punched him with a devastating im-pact.

He could wait for her now and test his control, or do the safer thing and leave.

The office screen door opened and closed, followed by the inside door.

"Leave it open, Keely. It's too hot."

"All right. Things are quiet at the cabins. I think they might all be asleep."

He didn't turn around, but continued to stare out into the night. "I doubt that. April's arrival will keep them going for most of the night."

She fussed with a light near her desk. "I didn't really thank you for taking down the hive."

He turned then and propped his shoulder against the wall, his thumbs hooked in the waistband of his jeans. "You're welcome."

"I thought Turk was going to do it. He told everyone at breakfast this morning that today was the day."

"Some people are allergic to bee stings. I didn't want to take the chance Turk might be one of them. And his enthusiasm about becoming your hero dropped considerably the closer he got to the hive."

"So you're my hero instead," she said softly.

The words sounded silly and mushy, and if he'd been facing her instead of watching the shadows cast by the desk lamp, she probably would only have repeated her thank-you. But he liked being called a hero. He liked being called a hero by her.

"Take off your shirt, Jed."

If she'd said strip, his reaction wouldn't have been more intense. Tell her the stings don't hurt. Tell her you ought to check on the boys, and she should be with April.

"April is up with Irma," she said, as though reading his mind. "After what you said about the boys bothering April, I thought while we were in here it would be a good idea to keep her with Irma."

"Yeah, a good idea."

"Jed? The shirt?"

"Listen, Keely, this is a lousy idea."

"I promise I won't try to seduce you," she said, as though not quite sure where the conversation might be going, but too curious to wait and find out.

Now was not the time to look directly at her. He didn't dare. He didn't want to see the promise in her mouth.

"You've been seducing me since I met you," he murmured, meeting her eyes anyway. He thought her mouth would keep the most erotic of promises.

The cap she'd unscrewed from the ointment tube slipped out of her fingers.

Jed stayed away. Safer. Colder and emptier, but safer.

He heard her swallow before she cleared her throat. In a too sedate tone, she said, "The more we talk about not doing anything, the worse it is. Take off your shirt. I'll put the salve on the stings, and that will be the end of it."

"You're right." He faced her on a raspy intake of breath. "Talking about it is probably worse than doing it."

"And there's a no-sex rule on the Island. People who make rules and then don't follow them themselves set poor examples."

"Lousy examples." He wondered if stripping in the director's office after hours was a good example. He peeled off the shirt.

Keely faltered.

In the low office light his skin appeared darker, the hair on his chest denser, the scar on his belly starkly prominent, more of a temptation for her mouth to soothe.

"Turn around," she said huskily, feeling such arousal shimmer deep in her.

She heard him swear, and for a moment she thought he was going to shrug back into the shirt and stalk out. Finally, he displayed his back. She envied his jeans for their closeness to his skin. His butt was flat, his hips slender. His wallet had left a white outline in the worn denim of the back pocket. A belt loop dangled by two threads.

She could offer to fix the loop, she thought. In fact, she could do it right now. There was a needle and thread in her desk....

"What in the hell are you doing?"

Her heart scampered up into her throat. "I was just—"

"Put the damn ointment on so I can get out of here."

To her stunned amazement, she felt tears in her eyes. She fumbled with the tube and squeezed too hard, getting enough of the white cream to do his whole back. She swallowed and grabbed some tissues.

Either the light was poor or her eyes were too blurry. "Jed, could you sit on the edge of the desk?"

He complied.

She didn't intend to look. She intended only to put the tissues in the trash. But when she lowered her gaze, she saw that the slight pull on the band of his jeans revealed no underwear.

"Jed?" She dropped the tissues into the wastebasket.

"What?"

She wanted to ask him why he didn't wear underwear. She'd noticed that fact at other times, like the day he pitched the tent. It wasn't really important, yet like everything about Jed, it took on importance because she was curious about him. She touched the small of his back, her fingers as light as a butterfly.

He glanced over his shoulder at her, his brows drawn into a frown. "Keely, do the salve, huh?"

"Oh, yes, the salve."

Quickly, she placed her hand on his shoulder. He jerked slightly as if the touch wasn't expected.

"Hurt?" she asked.

"Like hell."

"I'm sorry."

She didn't move her hand. She was absorbing the texture and strength beneath her fingers, liking that she had a reason to touch him. The stings were the size of quarters, darkish pink against his tanned skin. She gently massaged the cream around and around. She heard him suck in his breath.

"The swelling should go down," she said.

"Not likely."

"By tomorrow."

"Not unless I do something about it tonight," he countered.

His arm shot out, lifting her almost off her feet as he pulled her in one fluid motion to settle her between his legs.

"I can't stand it...." He groaned, his hands under her skirt, cupping her pantied bottom, drawing her in to him. Tighter. And tighter still. Then his mouth lowered onto hers with a sweeping hunger.

It was not a tentative kiss, nor was it tender. His tongue entered her, plunging deeply, taking everything she offered.

Keely held on to him, her own need to be close to him both acute and perplexing, but definitely irresistible. The ointment tube fell on the desk. She felt the buttons on his fly press against her stomach, and she eagerly coveted the strain on the denim.

He angled his head, trying to find more of her mouth, his hands selfish and wonderful on the flesh of her bottom. Keely looped her own hands around his neck, her fingers greedy to feel the black silk of his hair.

He touched her as intimately as their clothes-covered bodies would allow. He raised one of her legs high to ride along his thigh. Keely moaned when his hands moved up her back and under her sweater. His fingers grappled with bra hooks. She swallowed his curse with another kiss. She ran her own hands down his back to flirt beneath the band of his jeans.

The bra came loose, and when he cupped her breasts, his thumbs teased her nipples until she was overwhelmed by pleasure.

She sagged against him. "Jed...I think..."

"Easy, babe. I know. I've gotta stop." Yet even while he whispered the words, he slipped her sweater up and over her breasts. "I want to see you. I want to taste your skin on my tongue...."

And when the dim light revealed her creamy breasts and pink nipples, Jed closed his eyes and sucked in deep gulps of air. "God, this was a mistake."

She laid her hands on his cheeks, feeling the ragged breathing, drawing his mouth to her, sure she would die if he didn't ease the ache in her nipples.

"I can't, babe. There's no way I'll be able to stop there."

She whimpered, her hips agitated. Jed knew. He recognized the flush, the rising motion of her body, reaching.

"Keely, ah, babe..." He dragged her closer to his hardness, rocking her body against his.

She stiffened and tried to pull back, but he held her.

"This isn't how I want you. No, Jed..." But when he kissed her mouth, her protest died.

He promised himself only about fifteen seconds. Much longer and he'd lose it.

Her body arched. He held her, increasing the rhythm, watching her twist and lift as she crested. When her mouth parted, and her breathing was suspended, he pulled her up tight and swallowed the shudder of her release in a long deep kiss.

She lay heavy on him, spent and warm, her cheek moist and flushed against his chest, her hair tangled around his neck.

He didn't dare move. He knew he had to get out of there as soon as she got her breath.

Finally, she lifted her head and looked up at him. Had he ever seen green eyes gaze at him with such obvious pleasure? He wanted to capture the moment and hold it in his memory for the long cold nights ahead.

"Jed?"

She was going to talk about it. He saw the questions in her face; he watched her search for the right beginning. He wanted to get out and away. Far away where he could gulp in cold air.

He kissed her lightly and tried to disentangle her arms.

"Don't go. Please," she said softly.

"I need to check on the boys."

She didn't blink, as if she was afraid she might miss something. "You're angry, aren't you? That's never happened to me so fast, I mean without really making love...."

Jed groaned. "God."

Keely took rapid breaths. "It wasn't fair to you. I shouldn't have let you...."

He pulled her back into his arms. "I wanted you to. Shhh."

"It wasn't fair," she said again, this time with more conviction. "I mean, you . . . I could feel how hard—"

"Stop talking about it! You were hot and it happened," he growled.

She flushed, looking embarrassed. She moistened her lips. Jed once again set her away from him and got the shirt almost over his head when he saw her fumbling with her bra, a funny choking sound in her throat.

"Let me do it," he said roughly, throwing his shirt on the desk. "You hold your sweater up."

He ignored her wet sniffle, as well as the way she flinched when he touched her back. He swore when the hooks wouldn't catch.

"What's wrong?" she asked, trying to see over her shoulder.

"I bent the hooks."

"It's all right."

"It's not all right! It's all wrong. None of this should have happened. I shouldn't have been close enough to you to know what the hooks felt like."

He swore again and finally fastened the one hook that still worked. He jerked her sweater down and grabbed his shirt. "Let's go. I'll walk you to your cabin."

She sniffled once more. "I have to get April."

"Looking like that? Your hair is tangled, your cheeks flushed. Your mouth is wet and . . ." He couldn't say it.

"Swollen? Thanks to you," she snapped, angry now.

He didn't blame her. He wanted to tell her how beautiful she'd looked to him. How pleased he was that his touch brought her to fulfillment so fast. He wanted to hold her and soothe her and whisper sexy words and promises.

She dragged a brush through her hair, straightened her sweater and smoothed her skirt. "Thank God, it's dark."

He came to an instant stop by the door. To his amazement, her comment offended him. Not that he blamed her; for her sake he, too, was glad it was dark. Irma's seeing the Island's director looking as if she'd been tumbled and ravished wasn't a great idea. And April, who was probably sharper, would tease Keely. No doubt the word would get through to the staff as well as to the boys, who would chew it and relish it. But getting offended was a new reaction for Jed.

What had happened to her in his arms had meaning for him. He didn't like its being passed off as some shameful act she regretted now that the passion was cold.

Jed scowled. If he was offended, then he cared. Not just about what Irma or April might think, but about what Keely thought.

Yet before this new feeling had a chance to find a solid hold, another reaction seized him.

Dammit!

In his selfish need to kiss and touch her, he'd created exactly what he'd told her she'd done by bringing April to the Island.

He'd created a potential disaster.

Keely missed the bees' buzzing.

She lay on her bed, the moon watching her with a gentle eye, nudging her thoughts toward what had just happened in her office, and her resolutions to keep her relationship with Jed strictly business.

Very unprofessional conduct, she concluded now that she could think rationally. The objective voice inside her agreed, but the other voice, the one that kept her thinking about and wanting Jed Corey, told her that feelings shouldn't have to live by rules.

If only it were that simple, she thought with a grimace of disgust at the moon.

Facing him tomorrow would be the real test. She hoped she wouldn't stammer and blush. Well, maybe she'd refuse to meet those compelling gray and silver eyes.

It wasn't as though she were an innocent virgin unfamiliar with the throes of passion. Nor had she suffered an unsatisfactory sexual relationship with Paul. That was what concerned her. If she were sexually starved, or if she'd never met a man who could arouse her, then what had happened with Jed could be easily dismissed and forgotten.

But she felt intuitively that what had happened transcended sex and lust and hunger. Although those were there. God, were they there!

She rolled over, kicking the sheet back, her body hot and damp. She still tingled from the shuddering climax. Then she realized the experience went beyond the pleasure her body felt. That was only the surface. Her emotions during those intense moments had been born in her soul. And that meant caring and compassion and love.

In love with Jed Corey.

The whole concept was preposterous. She liked him. She thought he'd done a terrific job with the boys. And she had to admit they all looked up to him, although he called it sitting down with a fellow sinner.

Jed's comments about April being on the Island hadn't bothered her nearly as much as April's comments about him when she arrived. Freely, Keely admitted that April's "wows" had touched some possessive chord she'd never been aware of with other men.

She wasn't ready to call the feeling jealousy, and she refused to call it love. She was not in love with Jed.

Giving the moon another scowl, she bunched her pillow, searching for a cool place.

"Are you asleep?" April suddenly asked.

"Not yet."

"Do you still want to know where I got my earrings?"

Keely recalled asking April that question on the dock. At this point, with all that had happened, earring shopping wasn't high on her list of important topics. Listening to April, however, was important. "Sure."

A small giggle came from the roll-away bed. "From Bruce."

Keely grinned. So much for Bruce being a scumbag. "Oh? Well, I guess that shows he has good taste in earrings and in sports cars."

"Turk said they were cool."

Keely sat up. April was barely visible in the dark room. "When did he tell you that?"

"Tonight, out behind your office."

"The office? When were you out there?" Had April and Turk heard her and Jed? Keely wondered in dismay.

"After you took me to Irma's. She fell asleep and it was so hot I went outside. Turk must have been out walking, because he saw me. We didn't do anything, honest. We only talked."

Keely was sure the pounding of her heart was loud enough to alert the whole Island. "Turk was supposed to be in bed."

"He said he stopped at Jed's tent to tell him it was too hot to sleep, but I guess Jed wasn't there."

Keely didn't want to clear her throat and she didn't want to talk. Worse than April and Turk's hearing them would be their seeing them. A flash of her father's face, angry, disappointed and disgusted swam before her.

Keely coughed, got out of bed and went into the bathroom.

After drinking a glass of water she tested her voice in a tiny whisper. How could she have been so stupid? So unconcerned about not only the Island's rule of no sex, but her motives in coming here.

Looking at her reflection, she realized the depth of involvement it would take for her to fulfill her father's dream. More than words, more than a strong belief she could make the Island work, in fact an emptying of her own life.

For the Island, and for the boys and their problems, her father had sacrificed his personal life. Sacrificed it the way a priest gave himself to the church.

Could she do that? Could she turn her back on everything? True, her personal life hadn't been glitz and glamour and hunky guys, but she loved her beach house, her privacy and, yes, even the freedom to be attracted to a man like Jed Corey.

Apart from her mother, she had no family. She wouldn't be choosing troubled boys over her own child. She thought of Barbara Isherwood, choosing Bruce and his red car over April. Keely had been critical of her. Jed, too, had questioned Barbara's maternal instincts.

Keely felt that questioning her father's motives was tantamount to heresy, but she couldn't help it. Hadn't he done the same thing Barbara had done? His goals might have seemed worthier, loftier, but were they right? Was it ever right to neglect a child?

Keely had felt neglected by him, at moments even rejected. Like the day he'd forgotten to come home for her school's father-daughter banquet when she was in eighth grade, and the time she'd overheard someone telling her mother that Edgar must have wanted sons and that was why he preferred the rugged atmosphere of the Island to the white rugs and feminine charm of their home in Newport.

The rugged atmosphere that had helped boys like Jed. She thought of the abysmal background he'd conquered and the success he'd made of his life. Not in money or material things, but in living.

Edgar Lockwood had been a profound influence on Jed, and Jed made no secret of his fondness for Keely's father, a father he'd never had. She couldn't resent that, but she wondered if she was drawn to Jed because he possessed something that she believed her father had never found in his daughter.

She'd honestly never thought of Jed as a father figure, but she felt something. That had been all too evident a few hours ago.

She shivered, her mind clogged with thoughts that needed sorting.

Whatever her feelings about her father's treatment of her, they had nothing to do with her present responsibilities. And she should not allow herself to be distracted from those responsibilities by a sexual fantasy about Jed. Distance and reserve—those were both necessary these next few weeks, she decided as she examined her slightly swollen mouth. She'd maintain a professional attitude about doing the very best that she could do while she was here.

And afterward?

He'd go back to his apartment in Providence.

She'd return to her beach house in Newport.

Exactly the way things were before they met.

April stood in the bathroom doorway, her short nightie barely covering her thighs.

"Are you okay?"

Keely held the wet washcloth over her eyes. God, no. She was miserable. "I'm fine. Just hot, I guess."

April crunched the hem of her nightie. "I sorta like Turk."

Keely lowered the cloth, and tried for a not-too-concerned look. "Sweetheart, I don't think it's a good idea for you to get involved with Turk." Just as she shouldn't get involved with Jed, Keely thought sadly.

April tossed her head back, her eyes defiant. "Why not?"

"Because it will cause problems with the others." When she didn't respond, Keely asked, "You know what I mean, don't you?"

"I told you before, guys don't like me. They'll probably be glad Turk got stuck with me."

"I don't think that will be their reaction."

"So what am I supposed to do while I'm here? Live in this cabin like some hermit? I mean, jeez, it isn't like I'm doing anything weird with Turk. He just wants to be friends."

Keely sighed. Friends. She didn't believe that any more than she believed she and Jed could turn back their relationship to a simple friendship.

She put her arm around April and guided her back into the bedroom. "It's late. We can talk tomorrow."

"What about Turk?"

"I'll tell you what. You can see and talk to him at meals and during the day, but no more visits at night."

Back in her own bed, she glanced at the moon.

Could she take her own advice and do the same with Jed?

Chapter 9

In her office at her desk, Keely marked off the twenty-eighth day on her calendar. She drew the X over and over again with a black felt-tipped pen as though she could somehow trap time if she made the impression dark enough.

Her thirty-day trial period was nearing completion, and although she knew she'd done a credible job as director, she didn't feel very comfortable with the phrase *credible job*. It sounded too sterile and mechanical, and nothing at all like fulfilling her father's dream.

She knew that the board would consider her credible job and make a recommendation, and in all likelihood she'd remain as the Island's director. So why wasn't she bursting with enthusiasm? Why wasn't she pleased that the new house for the generator was complete, and the generator was installed and working? Why wasn't she happy that she could at least hold the beginnings of her father's dream in her hands? And why wasn't she grateful she wouldn't have to see Jed every day?

Jed.

She smoothed her fingers over the edge of her desk where he'd rested his hips, where he'd held her while she reached such an intense level of pleasure.

Two weeks ago. Yet she could still feel the deep pull in her womb.

After that night, she'd expected him to be distant or angry—overly kind, to prove they could remain friends, and that friends were all they'd ever be.

Actually, he'd been so even tempered, so professional, so accommodating whenever she approached him that she began to wonder if he'd forgotten what happened in the office.

Ridiculous, she'd told herself. He might not have gotten the pleasure she had, but he hadn't been uninvolved, either. He was the one who'd pulled her into his arms. But then, afterward, he'd withdrawn, almost as though he was afraid of what she'd seen and felt in him.

He was trying to hang on to his control. Jed and his damnable control.

It made her angry. Anger was unreasonable, she knew, but then reason hadn't been a big factor in anything that had happened between them. That anger simmered in her with the need to penetrate his control. To see if she could, at least once, make him act without thinking.

The confrontation had come a week after the passion in her office.

They'd played baseball, and the kids were sacked out on the grass drinking soda and eating pizza that Irma and April had made. Jed had walked in the direction of his tent, and she'd followed.

With her hair tangled and grass stains on her knees, she knew she looked more like a grubby kid than a woman who felt, at that moment, as if her entire personal life hinged on Jed Corey. She caught up with him in the clearing between her cabin and his tent.

"I don't appreciate you ignoring me," she said, suddenly breathing too hard.

Jed faced her, brushing dust off his jeans. His shirt had ripped when he'd slid into second base on a steal. She pretended she didn't notice that the button on his jeans was dangerously close to slipping out of its hole, and that he didn't wear underwear.

"I wasn't aware that I've ignored you. I congratulated you on that triple. You blew the doors off Snakeman when he thought he was gonna catch it and couldn't."

"I'm not talking about the baseball game."

Without hesitating, he unbuttoned his jeans and shoved his torn shirttail inside. Keely's gaze followed the methodical movements, her eyes focusing on the springy arrow of chest hair, following its aim down over his scar, past the opened fly, and what lay behind it. She felt a new layer of sweat break out on her forehead.

Jed slowly fastened the buttons. "You mean when you asked about the scrap pieces of wood and I was busy getting the generator clamped down? I'm sorry. I had to concentrate. When I looked up you were gone," he said in an unemotional but friendly voice that made her feel like a stranger who'd gotten lost and stopped to ask directions.

Perhaps lost isn't too farfetched, she thought. She planted one hand on her hip and flipped her braid back over her shoulder with the other while giving him her most annoyed stare.

"I want to make love with you, Jed." The bold statement tumbled out before she had a chance to give it too much thought. Or had she been thinking about it too much? Either way, she was tired and frustrated and the least he could do was not act so apathetic. And controlled.

His mouth twitched. "Don't you think this is a little public? Any one of the guys could walk down here and interrupt—"

"I don't mean here," she said candidly and loving the surprise she'd caught in his eyes.

"Your cabin, then?" he asked, and she wondered if there was such a reaction as serious amusement. "Or if you're really into roughing it, we could use the tent. It's a little small and not very soundproof if you're inclined to do anything more than moan your pleasure. But," he continued, a frown furrowing his brow and holding her with his eyes, "I recall there's a no-sex rule on the Island. Have the rules changed?"

"You are a bastard, Jed Corey."

"Yeah, I know."

"A cold cruel bastard."

"Who never should have touched you."

"Damn you! Damn you!" She flew at him; tears she didn't want to cry suddenly blurred her eyes. He grabbed her wrists, holding them, waiting until she ran out of breath and energy.

Finally, when her breathing slowed to a ragged rawness, he took her into his arms, cradling her, his breath whispering across her hair.

"Don't," she said on a hiccup. "I don't want you to comfort me."

But he held her, rocking her as though she were as precious and fragile as an irreplaceable object. She sniffed and hiccuped again and felt a rush of shame for her immature and foolish behavior. A thirty-year-old woman who possessed any pride wouldn't throw herself at a man. Certainly not at a man who obviously wasn't interested in catching her.

Now, as she recalled his giving her a light kiss on the forehead, and saying something about getting through their remaining time on the Island, she finally accepted what she'd known that night—that Jed would not allow himself to be anything more than the male presence she'd needed. Never would he be anything as intimate as a lover.

"Not one of your more professional moves," she muttered aloud, thinking of her boldness. His control apparently was stronger than anything he might feel for her. She sighed and walked over to the window. At least she wouldn't live with regrets.

She slipped her hands into the side pockets of her beige slacks. Her blouse, a light brown cotton with tiny buttons, was a little dressier than what she usually wore, but she was growing weary of jeans and shirts.

The day had been spent mostly in counseling sessions, and Turk was due in a few minutes. Keely held little hope that this session would be any better than the others she'd had with him. She'd spent time alone with each boy and had learned quickly that Turk wasn't the only bully. All these boys, although different in personality, had the impulsive need to dominate.

Needing a turf, Jed called it. He'd tactfully not mentioned April, although Keely grew more aware with each passing day of the tension surrounding the teenage girl. From the stirrings and the restlessness of the other boys, Keely had no doubt Turk had laid some sort of claim.

She picked up the folder on Turk and checked her notes from the last session. She'd talked about his need to wield power, to be fearsome and aggressive. Turk had spent most of the time in Keely's office watching the door that led to the eating area, in an obvious hope that April would appear.

She was in the kitchen now with Irma, and Keely could hear the two of them clanking pans and April occasionally laughing.

"I like cooking," April had told Keely one evening when they were discussing what April planned to do after high school. "Do you think I'm weird?"

Keely assured her she was not weird, and that in fact her preference showed maturity. Having positive likes and knowing how to focus gave a person a sense of purpose, a sense of seeing beyond the pleasure of the moment.

"Do people go to school to learn how to cook?" April had asked a few days later. "I mean, Mom puts everything in the zapper. You know, the microwave? Irma says she doesn't want to get nuked so she won't touch one. I asked Mom once to teach me how to cook, you know, like Irma does with real flour and a recipe? But she said women don't have to cook anymore."

Keely told her about cooking schools, but added that Irma would be an excellent teacher for a beginner. After talking to Irma, who said she'd be delighted to have April in the kitchen, Keely decided April's time would be better spent learning how to sauté peppers and onions than cleaning out office files.

She liked listening to the teenager's laughter. She was pleased at how she'd opened up, and except for the growing friendship—Keely privately referred to it as a relationship—with Turk, April seemed to have adjusted well to the Island.

Now Keely's attention was drawn to an argument outside over some leftover blocks of wood. Snakeman and Turk were circling each other like two wary predators. Jed stepped between them and sent Snakeman to pick up some tools. When Turk turned around, Keely saw one of April's earrings dangling from his ear.

He still had that swagger she'd encountered the day he arrived; it was more blatant now with April here. Jed hadn't said I told you so, but he'd grumbled something about cock of the walk, and that meant trouble.

Yet so far the skirmishes had been mild.

Keely turned away from the window, proud of herself, proud of her self-control around Jed. She only had to get through the next few days, then he'd be leaving and she'd put him out of her mind forever.

The board had yet to pay their unannounced visit, and she wondered if they'd changed their minds about it. Her reports had been detailed, and Judge Nelson had called her on the marine radio to tell her how pleased he was with them.

She'd worked and concentrated on her reasons for coming here, and from the results this past week she could say her efforts had paid off.

"Hey, baby, I'm here and I'm ready."

Keely turned from the window and gave Turk a long bored perusal. She'd perfected a rather laid-back attitude in regard to him. Self-preservation, she decided. His wildness, combined with his impulsiveness, hadn't changed so much as it had smoothed out around the edges. Given direction and some boundaries, she knew they could work in Turk's favor.

Keely motioned him to the chair by her desk. "You never quit, do you?"

"Only when I'm dead."

Endearing wasn't the word she would have used for Turk. "You have interesting taste in jewelry."

"Yeah? You like it?"

He slid the chair closer to her, and Keely felt a little like a steak dinner for a hungry wolf.

"Guess who gave it to me," he said with a snicker.

Keely folded her arms. "Snakeman?"

His frown was so sudden that she almost smiled. "You gotta be kiddin'. Yeah, you are." His laugh was a little nervous, a little leery. "Aren't you?"

"I'm kidding. Is that what the heavy words with Snakeman were all about? You wearing April's earring?"

He shrugged. "She gave it to me. What could I do?"

"It didn't occur to you to say you didn't want it?"

"Why should I?" He shoved his chin up and sprawled deeper into the chair, his legs spread open into a wide V. Keely knew Turk thought the lazy position gave him an air of authority. She read something else. He seemed more at ease with her than he had in earlier sessions, and he'd lost that get-out-of-my-business body language, although he still tried to say the words.

"All this talkin' crap about my life is a real bummer."

"So you've said at every session. Sometimes I wonder if the talking does any good."

"Like with me, huh?" he asked, trying to sound arrogant, but Keely heard in his voice a trace of hope that she wouldn't say yes.

"I admit you haven't been the easiest kid I've ever dealt with."

"Yeah? I'm tough. You know, I gotta be. The street ain't like no mama that gives a crap about you. Just when you think you got it together, you get chewed and screwed."

"Tell me, Turk. What does the street give you that you don't get at home?"

He shrugged.

Keely waited while he sat up and then sprawled out again. "I can take care of myself. I don't need no baby-sitter."

"Is that how you think of your mother? As a baby-sitter?"

"Mama? Nah, she's okay. Sometimes she pisses me off. Always cryin' about how I'm going to hell. She's . . . I don't know . . . she won't let me alone."

Interesting contrast, she thought. Mrs. Solitto and Barbara Isherwood. One worried too much. One worried not enough.

He glanced up, April's earring sparkling in the afternoon sunlight. "You let me alone. You don't bug me. How come she can't be like you?"

Keely hoped the expression on her face wasn't too emotional. It wasn't that she liked being preferred over his mother, but his comment was encouraging.

"I'm not your mother, Turk, and that may be the reason. While I care about you, and I want to help you get your life together, it isn't the same thing a parent feels."

"Yeah, I hate it when she cries and carries on."

He was quiet for a moment, arms folded across his chest. The usual arrogance slackened, leaving a young face that seemed vulnerable and regretful.

"Mama, sometimes, jeez, I don't know. She, uh, makes me feel like a real loser."

Softly Keely said, "I don't think that's her intent."
She told him about the letter his mother had written to
the court.

That seemed to amaze him. "Yeah? She told them
she needed me at home?"

"Yes."

"She ain't never told me that. She's always yellin'
about my freaked-out friends and how come I act bad.
I told her, bein' bad together is what kids do. Jeez, I
never knew she needed me, like, well, like she couldn't
get along without me." His glance at Keely waited for
a denial, for a word that he'd misunderstood.

"That's what she meant, Turk."

He chewed his lower lip. "A couple guys I know,
they're throwaway kids. You know what that means?"

She nodded. "Their parents threw them out and
don't want them back."

"I ain't got that problem," he said, without expecting an answer. Then she heard a new pride in his voice.
"April could, you know."

"April could what?"

"Her old lady don't care about what happens to her."

"Did April tell you that?"

"Sorta. She told me about some geek named Bruce,
and how her mother is screwin' around with him."

"It isn't a good idea for us to discuss April."

"I told her you were cool."

"Coming from you, Turk, I consider that a compliment."

He glanced around the office, his eyes coming back
again and again to the door that led into the eating area.
"I don't think it was a good idea you bringin' her here."

"You've been talking to Jed."

"Not about that. He just told us April, you know, her bein' a girl and all? And us guys, we, uh, well, we uh...get..." He fussed with a thread in his jeans, pulling it and smoothing it and finally breaking it. "Jed told us we better not screw things up for you. Uh, well, he didn't say screw, he said—"

Quickly, she interrupted. "I know what he said, Turk."

She glanced out the window to where Jed was directing the cleanup. She thought of the reports that had received so much praise from the board, and even though she knew the Island was no place for egos, she wondered if much of the success with the boys had really been Jed's and not hers.

Listening to Turk, she realized the depth of Jed's protective instincts. When he'd erected his tent she'd thought fleetingly that his obvious gesture of keeping the boys at bay went deeper. She'd sensed then that he wanted to protect her wish to fulfill her father's dream. His need to protect had extended to April, but again, it went beyond the girl and came back to her.

As though anything or anyone that hurt her...

"...make a move on her."

"I'm sorry, Turk. What did you say?"

"Them bums are itchin' to make a move on her."

Keely closed Turk's folder. "I'm not about to let anyone hurt April."

"If I had my lock back, then they wouldn't dare suck up her breathin' space."

Keely formed a picture of Turk with his lock-in-a-sock weapon. She harbored no doubts he could do some incredible damage.

"I ain't gonna let anythin' happen to her," he said, coming out of the chair and jamming his hands into his pockets. The jeans dragged down slightly.

He's like Jed, she thought, and his protective attitude toward April is like Jed's toward her. Like her father's protective attitude when he didn't want his family on the Island. Now Turk with April.

This was quite a change in attitude in the boy who'd arrived thinking only about himself. She wanted to rumple his hair. The side that had been shaved before his arrival had grown, giving him a soft young appearance. She wanted to hug him like a mother would hold her child, to tell him how proud she was of him.

But she didn't, knowing that at his age, it would only embarrass him.

He shuffled his feet, and moved the chair away from the desk.

Just then Seth stepped into the office from the eating area and glanced at Turk and then Keely.

"Sorry," Seth said. "Want me to come back?"

"It's okay, Seth, we're finished."

Seth gave Turk a suspicious look. She knew he didn't like Turk, hadn't liked him from the day he came to the Island. She'd listened to Seth's warnings, though they went too far with the suggestion that Keely send Turk back to be dealt with by the juvenile justice system. She pointed out that they'd already dealt with him and had had little success. When she asked Seth if her father would have given up on Turk, he agreed he wouldn't have. Neither would she. After today's session she was thankful she hadn't.

"Jed wants to see you, Keely-kid."

Her heart did a little jump that made her feel silly and girlish. She certainly should be beyond heart flutters and damp palms at the mention of Jed's name. He probably wanted to see her about her plans for the kids for the final two days.

She followed Seth to the door.

From behind her, Turk asked, "Hey, any soda in the fridge?"

"Help yourself," she answered as she left the office. She walked outside, across the grassless yard to where Jed was locking up the tools. Tommy walked toward them.

A few seconds later, Turk came out of the office, slamming the door.

"Irma says steaks are on for tonight," Seth said. He gripped Tommy's shoulder. "How about you helpin' me pick corn? Irma is fresh out of carrots."

Tommy grinned. "Sure." The two of them had formed a friendship over the past weeks. Keely smiled as Tommy followed Seth into the garden that lay behind the main building.

She glanced at a point over Jed's shoulder. "Seth said you wanted to see me."

His sweatband was damp, and the slight darkening on his cheeks indicated he needed a shave. He was sweaty and shirtless, and his jeans hung dangerously low on his hips. He doesn't own any underwear, she mused, no longer shocked and finding the idea incredibly sexy. His buttoned fly held the same intriguing challenge it had the night of the baseball game. She thought of Jed's comment about boys not being the only ones with dirty minds.

He turned around to pick up a ragged red T-shirt and pulled it on. Glancing at his muscled and very tanned back, she said, "The bee stings are all gone."

"Yeah. Your ointment did the trick. Let's go for a walk."

He quickly moved off toward the trees so that she had no chance to say no. The path they took led to the beach about four hundred yards away.

After they'd stepped out of the dense trees and stood overlooking the beach, they worked their way across the boulders and down to the cove of rocks called the Pirate's Den.

She was wearing sandals. They weren't too good for scrambling over sharp stones and slippery boulders, she decided after she almost slipped and Jed caught her. She took the shoes off and picked her way carefully in her bare feet.

"Do you think pirates really came in here and buried their treasures?" she asked, studying the rocks.

"And ravished their ladies."

"I never heard that."

"Because you aren't a teenage boy who feels deprived of sex."

The cove was shaped in an elongated circle, the rocks climbing high around them, shadowing the silent space underneath.

"Deprived like you?" she asked.

Jed propped his right shoulder against a smooth rock on one side of the entrance. Keely stood on the other side. She wondered if they looked like two sentries guarding the opening, or two people afraid to go inside and explore.

Jed glanced at her. The late-afternoon sun made it difficult to see his eyes. "No. I don't feel deprived of sex. I feel deprived of you." And before she could digest that, he added, "Which is what I want to talk to you about."

Deprived of you, she thought, her heart seizing the words, and loving their sound and meaning. "You don't waste words, do you?"

"Does that offend you? It shouldn't surprise you. Kisses and clutches in dark corners are not only frustrating but stupid for two adults."

"I agree."

He grinned. "Then this will appeal to you."

"I don't know if I want to know."

For a moment he appeared taken back, then straightened and walked a little deeper into the cove. Keely didn't follow him, but she felt the earlier flutter in her heart escalate into a drumbeat.

"Come here, babe."

The husky command was seductive. She glanced back toward the trees, but saw nothing except leaves swaying in the breeze. She felt a raw pull toward him, yet at the same time she knew if she stepped inside, she wouldn't come out the same.

Stalling, she asked, "What about the no-sex rule?"

"I don't recall mentioning breaking any rules."

"Don't play games with me."

"Considering what has happened between us, games are the last thing I want to play."

Keely was glad for the semidarkness of the cove, not so much because it covered her embarrassment, but because it hid her sense of joy and expectation. Like a gentleman, he didn't mention the night of the ball game, or even the passion she'd experienced in her office. But then she shouldn't be surprised. He never said what she expected. Admittedly, when he was the most blunt, the most truthful, it pleased her immensely.

She laced her fingers together, still reluctant to move into the cove with him.

"Keely?"

She dug her toes into the sand, the gritty grains squeezing between her toes. "I can talk to you from out here."

"You're not afraid, are you?"

Whether it was his words or the concern in his tone, she was reminded of that night at the beach house—Jed, stretched out on her couch, watching her, asking if she was afraid, then telling her what they were feeling was sexual chemistry. That night she'd sensed there was more between them. Much much more.

The sun poured on her back, urging her into the cool shadows of the cove. Urging her toward Jed.

"Afraid of you? No, of course not." But she was. Afraid she already cared too much about him to forget him when the time on the Island was finished.

He stepped out to the edge of the shadows, squinting into the bright sun. Without touching her, without looking at her, he murmured, "You were beautiful that night in your office. I want to see it again. I want to feel it again."

His gaze shifted suddenly to her as though he were looking for some reaction, some denial that she had felt beautiful.

Was this the way he'd felt that night? she wondered. Had he hidden it because he didn't know how to deal with it?

Vulnerable emotions expressed weeks later, but if he'd said those words right after what she'd experienced in his arms, she'd have been undone, preoccupied and incapable of doing the job she'd come to Black Horse Island to do. Beyond that, she'd probably have been filled with guilt about disappointing her father.

Jed moved farther out of the cove and into the light. His eyes drew her, making her feel as though he'd never looked at another woman in quite that way. It wasn't desire so much as hope, and yet she couldn't shake the sensation that there was wariness in his expression, too. As though he were preparing himself for an argument.

A sailboat moved across the water, its pink-and-white sail billowing in the wind. It looked so peaceful, she thought, watching the boat dip and rise. Yet inside her, beneath the dip and rise of her breathing, churned a steady and growing excitement.

Jed was beside her, his hand on her neck, his fingers burying themselves in her chignon. She jumped at the wanton shiver his easy touch sparked.

Then he whispered, his words making her eyes drift closed, her fingers tingle, her legs suddenly too weak to hold her. "I want you, Keely, but not here, and not on the Island. I want to be very private the next time. Just you and me and a long, long night."

Yes! Yes! She wanted to throw herself in his arms. But before she had a chance to make any response he murmured, "Please don't say no."

She was stunned at the plea that from anyone else would have sounded like begging. From Jed, the simple request acquired a haunting nuance, as if her refusal were his greatest fear.

"When?" she asked.

He sighed with what seemed to be relief. "The thirty days will be up the day after tomorrow. I want that night with you."

"One night?"

"Yes."

"And after that?"

He didn't say anything, once again not looking at her, almost as if he hoped she wouldn't need an answer.

She had to force herself to whisper, "There is no afterward, is there?"

He raked one hand through his hair. "No."

The word lay between them like a shroud. A sea gull cawed and landed on the beach.

She couldn't just accept "no." She couldn't. They'd come too far for that. "Why not?"

He glanced at her, looking somewhat stunned, she thought. "Don't turn into a counselor on me, babe. The chemistry has been between us since the day I came home and found you in my bed. One night will probably take care of it."

"Take care of it? You make it sound like the flu." She didn't turn away, but kept her eyes fixed on him.

"I can't give you anything more, Keely." He swore then, and she guessed he probably regretted beginning the conversation.

"How do you know if you don't try? You won't let go of your need to be in control. You care for me, I know you do. It isn't just chemistry. I think—no, I know. Yes, I know, I more than care for you. Why can't we see each other? I'm not asking you for anything more than that. I'm not going to try to maneuver you into marriage like Marcie did."

Keely felt a wall of frost instantly rise between them. His eyes clouded with anger. "How do you know about Marcie? Did Seth fill you in the way he did about the Judge and me?"

She crossed her arms, suddenly chilled in the warm breeze. She shook her head. "Not Seth. A cabdriver told me."

"A cabdriver? God! What were you doing discussing my life with a cabdriver?"

"I didn't discuss anything! He talked and I listened." She told him about Al's comments on the ride from Judge Nelson's office.

By the time she finished he'd moved back into the shadows. From the darkness he said, "Marcie is past history. You're nothing like her."

"I don't know if that's good or bad."

"She wanted more than I could give her."

So do I, she realized with an unexpected jolt. I want all of you. To Jed, she asked, "Marriage? Is that what she wanted?" She held her breath, expecting another barrage of anger.

"Yeah," he replied.

Keely wondered how one small word could indicate so much disillusionment. "You didn't dump her, did you? When Al told me that he made it sound like you were a monster. When you wouldn't marry her, she left you, didn't she?"

Keely waited for him to say something, anything. If she hadn't known he was still in the shadows of the cove, she would have thought he'd disappeared.

"Jed?" she called softly.

She stepped deeper into the darkness. He didn't move. He didn't try to touch her, or urge her closer. Keely could feel his tense wariness, as if he felt trapped.

Then, as if Marcie hadn't been the topic, he said in a husky voice, "One night, babe. Do we do it?"

She hesitated, then decided to let the subject of Marcie drop for the moment. "Yes. If you promise me one thing."

"No promises."

"Can't you at least hear it before you refuse?"

He sighed. "Do I have a choice?"

"No." She grinned at his patient frown. "I want you to promise me you won't close the door on us afterward and that you'll kiss me." She smiled. "Right now."

"That's two promises."

"Double or nothing."

"Kissing you messes up my head," he grumbled, as he cupped one hand around the nape of her neck.

"Was there a compliment in there somewhere?"

He began to open the tiny buttons of her blouse. "I get to choose where I kiss you."

"Jed, wait...."

He didn't, but then she didn't really want him to. She moistened her suddenly dry mouth, thinking about pirates ravishing their ladies.

The buttons were too many, and he seemed to linger on each one as though wanting to draw out the excitement of a long-wished-for gift.

"Most men would rip them off," she murmured, working the knot on his headband loose and then running her fingers through his hair.

"I'm trying to keep my primitive and savage thoughts about you under control."

Sparks of desire waltzed up her spine. "Tell me about them."

"No."

"When we make love?" She moved closer, eager to kiss him. "We can explore some of them."

His fingers stopped three buttons from completion, but she felt more than his physical hesitation; she felt him again withdraw emotionally. Was exploring his thoughts about her that disturbing to him?

His other hand cupped her hip and drew her forward. She resisted, weary now of trying to figure him out. "You know what you are? You're a coward. It has nothing to do with control. You're afraid to let out what you really feel. You're afraid to let me know that you care about me beyond protecting me because of gratitude to my father."

Gently he eased her closer. This time she didn't resist. He lowered his head and kissed the soft spot behind her ear. His words came softly, seductively. "I never said I didn't care for you. I don't make it a habit of lusting about a woman I don't like."

She tried to concentrate on what she wanted to say, not on what his mouth was doing to her ear. "Don't generalize with me, Jed. I know you don't think I'm some vague woman you can easily forget. You lived with Marcie, and I can't imagine you living with a woman if you didn't care deeply for her."

He lifted his head, and looked at her. "So now we're back to Marcie."

Keely tipped her head to the side, watching him watch her. "You did care for Marcie, didn't you?"

"Deliver me from questioning women," he murmured under his breath. "She was fantastic in bed. Okay? That answer your question?"

"No."

"Hell." He stepped completely away from her.

She ignored the urge to pull him back. "What I asked before is right, isn't it? She did leave you."

She saw the fury in his eyes and considered withdrawing. Yet she felt as if she'd hit the edge of some dark thought Jed didn't like to face. To her amazement she felt an exuberant gratitude to Marcie. If Mar-

cie had been determined enough she might have ended
up married to him.

He let out a deep breath. "Yeah, she left. I didn't try
to stop her. She got just what she wanted. A husband,
a couple of kids, a picket fence and a gas grill in the
backyard. The all-American family. Satisfied now?" he
asked, waiting. But the frown on his face told her she'd
better be satisfied, because he was done talking about
Marcie.

He opened the last three buttons of her blouse. Keely
slipped her arms around his neck.

He eyed her suspiciously.

"No more questions," she murmured.

"Thank God."

He didn't reach behind her to unhook her bra; he
simply lifted her breast from the lacy beige cup and
lowered his head.

Keely's moan of pleasure escaped before his lips
moistened her nipple. She tipped her head back; the
sensation of his hot mouth startled her body into feeling a mass of delicious spins and whirls.

The rock beneath her feet suddenly felt slippery, or
were her legs getting wobbly? Her hands gripped his
shoulders, her nails digging deeper as he pulled her
nipple into his mouth. Savage sweetness tore through
her body; her arousal spread deeper and fuller.

He leaned back against the wall of stone and lifted
her up to ride his thigh. Keely moved her leg to settle
against him and was rewarded not only with his hard
arousal but a low groan.

"This is crazy, you know, putting ourselves through
this torture," she said breathlessly.

"Tell me about it," he growled. He gave both breasts a very wet kiss, his hands fascinated with their shape and response. "God, I want you," he murmured.

If they continued, despite the rule of no sex, despite the rocks and knowing that everyone would wonder what had happened to them, she knew this time it would be impossible to stop.

Yet as much as she wanted him, as much as she loved the intense excitement that leaped between them and the promise of total fulfillment she knew his body would provide, she realized they had to stop. She wanted him when there were no deadlines, no possibility of an embarrassing interruption, no excuses to hold back.

As he lowered his head and nuzzled her breasts, she said, "Two days will seem like forever."

His agreement never came. All they heard was April's scream.

Chapter 10

Keely tore herself away from Jed. Terror raced through her as she ran from the cove into the sunlight and up onto the rocks leading back to the trees. Jed followed, his stride long and sure.

"Where the hell are your shoes?" he shouted when he suddenly realized she was barefoot.

Trying to button her blouse while she ran, she stumbled on the rocks. "Up farther. I took them off before I got this far. Ouch!" she cried when she stubbed her toe.

"You picked a dandy time to go barefoot."

"And you picked a dandy time to climb on the rocks." She winced, fighting her tears, her terror at what had made April scream, and she damned her sandals for not being where she thought she'd dropped them.

Jed swore. Without coming to a complete stop, and with surefooted grace, he scooped her up in his arms as if she weighed no more than a seashell. He crossed the last of the rocks and headed back toward the path.

Neither said anything, their fear and concern for April obvious in their rush to find her. Jed dropped Keely on her feet when they reached the trees.

"It sounded like it came from the cabin area," he said, running in the rough terrain alongside the smoother path. He dodged a rotten tree trunk.

"When I left with you, she was in the kitchen helping Irma," Keely said, more to reassure herself that she hadn't shirked her responsibility in order to be with Jed. But her thoughts chanted the real truth.

She'd blown it.

She was responsible.

She'd made her father's dream a nightmare.

"It's not her scream that worries me so much as what she's screaming about." Jed took Keely's arm as they reached the clearing near her cabin.

"Oh God!" Keely breathed out the words like a supplication, her legs, so strong in her frenzy to get here, now felt like soft putty. Her fingers dug into Jed's arm.

He removed her tense hold, giving her hand a reassuring squeeze. "Stay here," he told her.

Irma, with flour on her apron, was standing there saying, "Please stop, please stop...."

The person closest to Keely was Tommy. He had one arm wrapped around April. She was crying. Keely felt a profound relief that April was only crying. The rest of the staff were trying to control the boys, who showed their divided loyalties by shouting and screaming at the scene before them—Snakeman and Turk, rolling on the ground, fists jabbing at each other.

Seth and Marvin were attempting to separate the fighters and not get hit. Keely saw blood on Turk's face.

Jed stepped into the melee. ''All right. Enough. Break it up.''

Neither paid any attention. The fear on Seth's and Marvin's faces changed to relief at the sight of Jed.

Jed reached down and grabbed Turk's arm.

Turk reared back. ''Get away from me, man!''

Snakeman took advantage of the distraction and twisted Turk's arm until Keely was sure she heard something snap. Turk yelled. April screamed again.

Keely started forward. ''Stop it! Both of you!''

Then Turk pulled a knife.

Jed froze. Seth and Marvin stumbled backward. Keely gasped.

Turk scrambled up, gripping the knife in his right hand. Wincing, he straddled Snakeman. Turk darted a quick glance at April, his concern for her obvious. His face was pale from the painful twisting of his arm by Snakeman. He swung the silver blade slowly back and forth a few inches from Snakeman's belly.

His voice low and steady, Jed said, ''Give me the knife, Turk.''

''No way.''

Keely moved closer until she stood only a foot behind Jed. He kept his eyes riveted on Turk as he said, ''Get back, Keely. Everyone stay back. We don't need any heroes.'' Then he crouched on his haunches. ''What gives, kid? What's the problem?''

Snakeman growled. ''I'm the one with the problem, man. Get that knife before he cuts me.''

''Shut up,'' Turk snarled.

Snakeman came back with an expletive that Keely had never heard.

Turk swallowed. When he turned his head, she saw that April's earring had been cruelly torn from his ear.

"He touched her, man. I warned him."

Jed glanced over at April. Tommy had loosened his hold. "You okay, sweetheart?"

April's face was wet with dirt and tear-streaked mascara. Her blue blouse was torn and she'd wrapped her arms around herself to keep the front panels together. She sniffled and nodded, but her attention was all on Turk. Keely moved over beside her. April started to cry again and Keely drew her into her arms.

"Shh. Are you sure you're okay?" she asked in a soft whisper.

"Turk's the one who's hurtin'." April's statement was followed by fresh tears.

Jed spoke to Turk in a soothing voice as though the two of them were telling street stories. "This is no good, kid. I know it feels right, but there's too much at stake."

"It's his fault. Tellin' me she's puttin' out, then tearin' her clothes, tryin' to move on her. He asked for it, man."

Jed stared down at Snakeman. The kid whose lazy movements had become so familiar was now stiff with fear. "Did you move on April?" Jed asked with a brutal coldness.

Snakeman seemed to shrink. "Hey man, I didn't mean nothin'. Get him away from me. He's gonna cut me."

Keely moved up behind Jed. "Turk."

Jed snapped, "I thought I told you to stay back."

She ignored him. "April is frightened, Turk. Frightened for you."

"I can take care of myself," Turk said, his voice stronger, the knife still in his hand.

"She's afraid she won't ever see you again. This kind of behavior here on the Island means you'll be sent to the training school. No second chances, Turk."

"And what was I supposed to do? Let him put his hands on her?"

Keely glared down at Snakeman, who grumbled, "I don't remember no one sayin' he had all the rights."

Jed said, "Defending April was right, Turk, but the knife is bad news. Let's have it."

Turk regarded Jed with a suspicious look. The silvery steel knife glistened as he turned it slowly in his hand, as if allowing his imagination to run over all its potential. Then he glanced at April. That was a mistake.

Snakeman moved. Jerking upward, using his fist, he knocked Turk's knife hand.

"Turk!" April yelled.

Turk fell off Snakeman, who reached for the knife. Jed stepped on his wrist, lifting his boot only when the teenager yowled with pain.

Keely helped Turk to his feet. Murmurs and shuffling sounds could be heard as the staff moved the rest of the boys away from the scene. Irma waved her apron as though to clear the air. Seth looked as if he were in shock.

April rushed over to throw herself at Turk. "You're bleeding and all bummed up."

"Yeah." Keely heard pride and gallantry in the single word. Turk wrapped one arm around April's neck.

"Perhaps, Ms. Lockwood, you would care to explain what we've just witnessed?"

Everyone came to a pulse-pounding stop.

Keely's first thought was that five dry-cleaned bureaucrats had come to pass judgment on the masses.

The board members stood in a shoulder-to-shoulder line at the edge of the clearing, as if they'd be corrupted if they got too close. Keely closed her eyes. Please, she prayed, let this not be happening.

Jed picked up the knife, closed it and slipped it into his pocket. "Terrific timing," he muttered sarcastically.

Judge Nelson looked grieved as if someone had died.

The social worker, a middle-aged woman named Ellen Rivera, wore a pained expression, as if what she'd just witnessed made every other state social program look bad.

Dr. Lewis, whom Keely knew only as a psychologist from Barrington, adjusted his rimless glasses as if considering using the incident in a report for a scientific journal. He leaned toward Ellen, who nodded unceasingly as if her neck had come unhinged.

John McGovern, Keely's dinner date in May, was sparse-haired and on the twilight side of sixty. When he was governor he had appointed Keely's father to the bench. Even across the hundred feet or so that separated them, Keely could see the disappointment in his eyes. John and Judge Nelson had been her strongest supporters.

John stood next to the last member of the board: Virginia Foote, who had raised the loudest objections to Keely's becoming the director. She'd come on the board three years before Keely's father died. Keely had heard Judge Lockwood call her a "starched moralizer in an orthopedic hat." The hat the Judge had referred to was a black felt cloche that did indeed look as if it held her head on straight. She carried a roomy purse that Keely guessed contained at least one vial of smelling salts.

It was Virginia Foote who had spoken.

Jed leaned close to Keely. "Wing it, babe. By the looks of them, explanations aren't gonna cut it."

Keely wiped her hands on her slacks. Her blouse had been pulled out, but she silently thanked a merciful fate that she'd gotten it buttoned. Regretfully, she admitted to herself that her disheveled appearance was unimportant compared to the scene before the board members. Fighting. A knife. Blood.

And then there was April, here by no authority other than Keely's. The folly of her decision weeks ago on Aquidneck Dock appeared to her now with objective clarity. Bringing April here because she had no choice was one thing, but keeping her here was another. So was making no attempt to find someone to take April, not calling Judge Nelson and explaining about the teenager when she knew the board would be making an unannounced visit, ignoring Jed's warning that there would be trouble. Keely squeezed her eyes shut.

Had she thought that circumventing the board, and violating the contract the Island had with the state, was justified because of one girl? Had she thought that as director she was as invincible as her father had been?

Bleakly, she realized that she'd not only acted without considering the consequences, but she'd based her decision on what she'd felt was her infallibility.

She rubbed her fists into her closed eyes. My God, she thought. She'd turned her own dream into a nightmare.

Judge Nelson came forward, his face a sickly white. His glance went from Snakeman crouched on the ground, to Turk, to April, and finally settled on Keely. The board won't overlook this, his eyes told her.

He gave Jed an angry scowl. "Corey, this was the sort of thing you were here to prevent."

Keely had to pull herself out of a quagmire of muddled thoughts to say, "Don't blame Jed. It wasn't his fault."

Judge Nelson regarded her from under a frown. "You're not defending him?" he snapped as if she'd said the worst possible thing. "Of course it was his fault. As it is yours. Even without a knife fight, the presence of this young woman," he said, glancing at April, "is enough to cancel your directorship." He took Keely's arm with a too gentle and too calming touch, as if she might fly into hysterics, and said in a low voice, "How did she get here and why?"

Keely swallowed. "I brought her here."

To Keely, his expression could only be described as dumbfounded, then disappointed. Before he could begin listing the implications of what she'd done, she shook his hand away. "Turk needs some first aid on his ear."

Turk winced when April touched his lobe. Jed said nothing. Keely could hear his breathing and drew some calmness from its even rhythm.

Judge Nelson was staring down at her feet. "Where are your shoes?"

The rest of the board members surged closer, reminding Keely of seaweed on an incoming tide.

She, too, stared down at her feet. They were dirty, and when she thought about why, and where she'd been, and April, and the knife, and Turk's bleeding ear, she wished for one instant that she'd stayed in her nice safe office in Providence and shuffled papers.

Then she took a deep breath and spoke to the board members, meeting the eyes of each one directly. "I know you have many questions. If you'll give me a few minutes, I'll meet you in my office and I'll try to answer them." Her own steadiness amazed her. Inside, she felt a hurricane of emotions.

"I told the board this was an inappropriate appointment," Virginia Foote said. "And as for that Corey person—" she spoke as if Jed had already been dismissed "—he looks more like trouble than these poor boys."

Jed helped Snakeman to his feet. Turk glared at his onetime friend.

Snakeman shrugged. "Hey man, no broad is worth this crap."

"She ain't a broad!" Turk yelled. "Come near her again and I'll cut off your—"

Virginia Foote seemed to rise into her cloche hat. One hand went over her mouth in horror, while the other clutched her purse.

John McGovern took hold of her elbow. "Why don't we wait in the office." He led her away toward the main building.

Jed sent all the boys but Turk into their cabins.

Seth walked over to Keely. "I'll bring the first-aid kit," he told her with a troubled and guilty shifting of his feet. "I should have been keepin' an eye on things, like Jed said. Jed and me, we both knew trouble was brewin'. If it'd been only a fight, well, the board wouldn't be so angry. But a knife!" He said the word as though a knife's existence on the Island came by evil spirits. "Where did Turk get the knife?"

"The knife was mine," she said quietly, and then damned herself for saying it with Judge Nelson so close. They were all in enough trouble without her adding the knife to it. The judge gave no indication that he heard her, but that didn't mean anything. Judges had a sixth sense about when to react. No doubt, if he'd heard, it would come out in a long tedious lecture before this episode was over.

Poor Seth, she thought. Her words had made his face even grimmer than it had been when the fight was going on.

"Yours?" he croaked. "What are you doing with a knife like that? It's a switchblade!"

"I know what it is," she snapped, thinking of her childish act of bringing the switchblade as some silly talisman to show Jed Corey she could handle herself. Right, she thought, with a growing disgust at the mess she'd created. She couldn't even handle Jed.

She laid her hand on Seth's arm. "It's a long story, Seth."

He patted her hand with a distracted but fatherly affection. "Did Jed know you had that knife? I don't ever remember your dad thinking he needed weapons to keep the kids in line. I don't know," he said with a confused sigh. "I thought this would all work like it did when your dad was here. I thought it would all be the same."

A memory flashed into Keely's mind—that day in Jed's apartment when she'd asked him why he wouldn't come with her. He'd said: "Have you ever heard 'To every thing there is a season. A time to be born, and a time to die'? The Judge was the season for the Island. When he died, the Island died."

She'd hated his words, denied them. *Had* the Island died when her father died? Had her determination to fulfill a dream grown from a selfish need to prove she could make the Island work as it had before her father's death?

Seth shuffled off, seeming older, discouraged, disappointed.

"Ellen?" Judge Nelson urged the social worker forward. "Take this young lady up to the office with you."

April backed away from Ellen and clung to Turk, her pleading eyes on Keely. "No. I want to stay with Keely. You can't make me go with her."

Judge Nelson sighed. "Keely, please?"

Keely took April's arm and urged her aside. "Sweetheart, I'm not going to desert you. Go up to the office with Ms. Rivera, and as soon as I get Turk fixed up I'll be there."

More tears leaked from April's eyes. "You promise? You won't leave me?"

Keely took the sobbing girl into her arms. "I can't make a promise, April. I don't know what will happen." At April's frantic head shaking, Keely said, "Listen to me. You don't want me to lie to you, do you? I'll do everything I can, but as you can see, I don't have a lot of clout at the moment."

April looked at her a long time, the fear in her eyes changing to frustrated anger. In a choked whisper, she said, "You were making love with Jed, weren't you? That's how come you weren't here. That's how come you look all mussed up. You know what? You're just like my mother. Just like her..." She pushed Keely away, crying harder now, stumbling.

Keely's brain felt numb. She lowered her head and took deep breaths.

A hand cupped the back of her neck, a thumb feathering over the slamming pulse. Soothing, familiar, the fingers kneading.

His words were whispery and gentle. "If it wouldn't make everything worse for you, I'd take you in my arms."

"Oh Jed, how could it be any worse?" She wanted his arms, his strength, his solid control to keep her from flying into a zillion pieces.

"Come on, babe. You're the Judge's daughter. You're not gonna let a bunch of bureaucrats blow away your dreams, are you?"

"I've blown away the dreams all by myself," she said miserably.

His fingers continued their gentle motion. She glanced up at him. He stopped and laid his hand against her skin, warm and reassuring. His gray eyes were softer now, full of encouragement.

Then, as though they were the only two people on the Island, she slipped her arms around his waist. His skin was slightly damp, the muscles in his back tight. She held him as if he alone defeated the nightmare, as if he alone completed her dreams.

Jed stiffened slightly. "Babe..."

"Hold me, please," she murmured. "Just for a minute."

He relaxed and let her rest against him. Their embrace wasn't sexual; neither did it show anything to the onlookers but a sense of one human being drawing support from another.

Finally Keely withdrew her arms, and Jed stepped away from her.

Judge Nelson glanced from one to the other. Seth came back carrying the first-aid kit, which he handed to Keely.

The judge said to Seth, "I want you to call the marine operator, and get hold of Walt Danner. Tell him I told you to call, and that I need some people from the juvenile authorities over here to take these boys off the Island.''

Keely interrupted, her eyes wide, her face pale. ''You're going to send them all to the training school, aren't you?''

''Only temporarily.'' At her protest, he held up his hand to indicate there was no point in arguing. ''You know I have no choice. The Island will be closed at least until after the inquiry. I can't just release these kids on the street. Neither the board nor I have that authority. The court will make the final decision.''

Keely lowered her head and nodded. There wasn't an alternative, she knew, but she hated it.

Seth nodded and walked back toward the main building. Judge Nelson instructed the staff to help the kids get their stuff packed. He told Dr. Lewis and Ellen Rivera to go on up to the office.

They filed away like robots, Keely thought. April went with Ellen, but not with any enthusiasm.

''Corey, get your things together,'' Judge Nelson said, sounding as if he were issuing a decree from the bench. ''The ferry is still docked. I want you on it and out of here. An inquiry will be scheduled, of which you'll be notified. I expect you to be there. Be prepared to explain your actions at that time.''

Jed didn't move, but when Keely glanced at him she saw his steel-eyed glare. Perhaps it was her imagination, but she was sure she felt a closing down of all his emotions. Emotions that she'd only begun to tap into, emotions she knew he needed to explore.

He was blaming himself for today, she knew, for the heat they each had aroused in the other. But she understood, too, that beyond all that he probably felt he'd betrayed her father, given back disaster instead of gratitude.

"Wait, please," Keely protested. "You can't make Jed leave."

Judge Nelson gave her a stern look. "I beg your pardon. I have the official authority, Keely, and I cannot shirk my responsibility by exercising the indulgent grace of your father's friend. What the board and I witnessed is inexcusable. Your admission of owning the switchblade—frankly, I find that quite shocking. Instead of helping these kids your actions, or inaction, have probably contributed to their problems."

Jed moved closer to Turk, saying something to which Turk nodded.

"That isn't fair," Keely shouted. "You don't know what led up to what you saw. Turk was defending—"

Nelson held his hand up. "You'll have plenty of time to explain yourself at the inquiry. Get the young man's ear cleaned up. We'll stop at the emergency clinic on the mainland. Corey, I thought I told you to get your stuff together."

Jed's voice was low and cold. "The knife was mine."

Keely stared at him, blinked rapidly, then grabbed his arm. "No, Jed, listen—"

He shoved her away. "Turk'll back me up."

"Jed! My God, why are you doing this?"

He swung on her. "Shut up!"

Keely opened her mouth and then closed it, stunned by the fury in his words. She'd never heard him so angry.

Jed was back facing Nelson. "Did you hear what I said? I don't want any stiff-shirted board filleting her, do you hear me?"

Judge Nelson took a step backward, appearing a little disoriented as though he'd roused a sleeping demon. Coldly, he said, "You're hardly in a position to give orders, Corey."

Jed let out a long labored breath. "But you'll agree that her father wouldn't want that, either."

The judge rubbed his chin and finally nodded. "All right. I'll see if I can persuade them not to blame her for the knife."

He peered at Keely with some uncertainty, and she knew he felt an obligation to her father's memory.

"I'm perfectly capable of being responsible for my actions," she said in a clipped voice. "Don't listen to him. He's trying to protect me." She glared in Jed's direction, but he'd begun to take down the tent.

It seemed that as far as Jed was concerned, it was ended. Fleetingly, she thought of the one night he'd wanted with her. She supposed that, too, was now only a hopeless dream.

Jed moved with a determined efficiency as if he wanted to get away from her quickly. He was obviously very upset by her refusal to allow him to take the blame for her stupidity.

Nelson seemed more than willing to believe Jed. The judge had always subscribed to sexist rules—knives belonged to the guys, women used Mace and whistles. Keely almost laughed. Jed had said much the same thing, but from Jed, she thought it was amusing. Nothing that had happened, and nothing Judge Nelson had said was even remotely amusing.

Jed wouldn't look at her, or maybe she'd simply become someone he'd dismissed from his life, the way he'd dismissed Marcie when she walked out on him.

Keely knew Jed didn't need her. Strange, she thought, how she'd resented the way her ex-husband had tried to tie her to him, and yet with Jed, she desperately wanted to be part of him. Perhaps there was a difference. She'd never been part of Paul, but more of a convenience to him.

Hadn't she told herself repeatedly she had no time to nurture a relationship with a man? Well, she thought in disgust, that shouldn't be a big problem now. There was no man and no relationship.

"Keely," the judge said. "The young man's ear?"

She dragged her attention away from Jed and back to Turk. "Yes. Come on, Turk."

One thing she did intend to do, she decided as she took Turk into her cabin; she would convince the board the knife was hers.

In the small bathroom, she cleaned and dried Turk's earlobe. "You took the knife from my handbag, didn't you?"

He winced at the first touch of antiseptic. "I didn't know you had it. I was lookin' for a nail file. My ma always carried a nail file. I knew Snakeman was gonna try somethin' with April."

She could hardly chew him out for defending April. She'd last seen the switchblade the day she went to see Judge Nelson. She'd pushed it aside to get her wallet to pay the cabdriver. "You took it this afternoon when you stayed in my office to get a soda, didn't you?"

"Yeah. Ouch! Hey, that stuff's making it hurt worse."

"Why did you lie to Judge Nelson?"

"Jed told me to back up whatever he said."

"When we get to the office, I want you to tell them the truth."

"No way."

"Turk . . ."

He shook his head, the smell of the antiseptic strong in the air. "Hey, Jed'll fry my butt. Look, it ain't no big deal. What are they gonna do to Jed besides give him some runaround that won't amount to nothin'. They ain't never gonna believe a classy lady—" He grinned. "That's what Jed says you are. Anyway, they ain't gonna believe the knife was yours." The grin shrank to a frown. "Hey, I thought I was seein' things when I saw the blade."

Keely closed the first-aid kit and washed her hands. "Lies are a lousy defense, Turk. And as far as Jed frying your butt, that was just a threat."

"Hey, you don't know Jed Corey. He don't make threats. Oh, he wouldn't kill me or nothin' but hey, I don't need him on the wrong side of a favor. You never know when you need a guy to back you up. And Jed, he's the kind of guy you want with you, not against you."

"Street loyalty."

"Yeah, ain't that what I said?"

Keely sighed. She'd just have to convince the board herself. A call to Debbie to ask her to recount what happened in the office with Sean and the knife would be a start.

"Turk, about what Judge Nelson said."

He stared at his unlaced sneakers. "Yeah, it stinks."

"The knife fight might work in your favor, because you were defending April."

He gave a disgusted snort. "Yeah, right. Like they're gonna believe me."

"I'll do what I can at the inquiry."

He shrugged. "Thanks."

They walked out of the cabin, Turk a little in front of her. A lone bee buzzed. Searching for the missing hive, she guessed sadly, her own thoughts about bees and stings and a very sexy back making her even sadder.

The tent was down. The space looked too empty, the distance between her cabin and the boys' too open, too stark.

Jed wasn't around. His duffels lay nestled together as though they were trying to hide something from prying eyes.

"I was just wonderin'..." Turk swung back toward her, his grin a little too intimate.

"What is it?" she asked warily, not even caring if the loneliness that crept through her could be heard in her voice.

"Uh, were you and Jed, uh, well you know, gettin' it on?" He peered at her bare feet, her dusty slacks and then at her wrinkled blouse. At her sudden intake of breath, he said quickly, "Hey, stay cool. It ain't exactly a secret he's got the hots for you."

Had the board come to the same conclusion?

She sent Turk to his cabin and the staff member waiting there, while she went back into her cabin to do some repair work on her appearance.

Feeling less vulnerable in a clean sweatshirt, jeans, sneakers and her hair back in a braid, she stood in the office a little while later, feeling the stuffiness, not from the summer heat but from too many people in a small place.

She listened wearily as the members of the board, one at a time, gave their opinion of what they'd seen.

Irma had poured coffee and served wedges of strawberry shortcake as though the board were there for a social visit. Keely managed a smile when Irma whispered, "It's going to be okay, I know it."

While they were eating, she thought, they couldn't talk. But that proved not to be so. John McGovern commented that with cooking this good, it was no wonder the kids looked so healthy.

"April made the shortcake," Irma said proudly, and all eyes turned to April, who had moved her chair closer to Keely's. She sniffled, her cheeks pink at the sudden attention.

"Yes, the girl. No explanation has yet been given for her presence," Virginia Foote said, as though Keely had created a spicy atmosphere for sin.

Keely told them why she'd brought April to the Island and to her relief saw that both Judge Nelson and John McGovern tentatively agreed she'd made the right decision given the situation.

Dr. Lewis furiously took notes.

In a squeaky voice, Ellen Rivera added, "The state will never approve, you know. The contract with the Island might be terminated. Mixing the sexes is not good policy."

By the time Virginia Foote finished her say, Keely felt as though she'd been filleted, sautéed and burned. No one mentioned the hug Keely had given Jed, but she guessed the action simmered and bubbled in at least three minds.

Virginia Foote declared there would be no further discussion on the matter. Keely would be expected to give a full explanation at the official inquiry of April's presence and the knife fight.

Keely stood and went to the window. She heard the low hum of the new generator inside its wooden house.

She'd spent a good part of her days here at her desk watching the progress out this window. Watching Jed.

Jed directing the carpentry. Patient when the kids nailed the boards wrong. Enthusiastic when Tommy and Turk correctly measured and cut the lumber for the floor.

Now she saw Jed walking not toward the office, but toward the ferry dock. Leaving the Island. Leaving her.

He wore the same buttoned jeans and raggedy red shirt. One duffel was slung over his shoulder. He carried the other one by a handle. She envied their closeness to him. His walk was steady and solid as though his destination were irreversible, even if she ran out and flung herself in his arms.

Behind her, the board members murmured. She heard Judge Nelson say something about "that can wait for the inquiry," and found herself not caring about what decision they made.

Sadness caught in her throat. Her gaze soaked up Jed, selfish for every nuance of him. His protectiveness. His control. His deep sense of caring.

She felt shallow with her talk of fulfilling dreams, when Jed, all the while, had seen the reality behind her dream.

Perhaps the problem lay not with the dream, but with who possessed it. Sharing dreams was one thing, but no one could step into another person's dreams and make them work. Her father's vision of an Island for troubled boys hadn't been hers. Hers had been to connect somehow with her father, to discover exactly what magic this Island had held for him.

She must have known what she was doing. She wasn't stupid; neither was she dense when it came to probing into deeper motives. Probably she'd been deliberately blind to what she didn't want to accept.

From the beginning she'd been caught up by the wispy idea of making herself acceptable to her father by continuing his work. Fulfilling dreams or spawning a nightmare? One look around the office answered that question for her.

The ferry horn pumped, signaling it was leaving.

Jed was leaving.

She rested her shoulder against the window frame, her fingers cold, her heart beating with a hollow thump.

She wanted to cry. She wanted to run after him. She wanted to hate him.

She closed her eyes. Her father had loved Jed Corey. So did she.

Chapter 11

Keely brought her office calendar home and hung it in the kitchen on the pineapple-shaped bulletin board beside the telephone. The black Xs stopped abruptly at day 28, as if something in her life had died then.

She sat at the butcher-block kitchen table stuffing containers and balled-up napkins from a fast-food lunch into the carryout sack.

Across the kitchen, April slouched unenthusiastically against the wall, the telephone pressed to her ear. Barbara Isherwood was obviously doing all the talking. April grumbled an occasional "yeah."

Keely, herself, didn't feel much better than the teenager.

She'd been unable to convince the board that the switchblade was hers, which made her angry because they insisted on assuming the worst about Jed. They hadn't quite called her a liar, but Virginia Foote had phrased it quite eloquently, accompanied by her gimlet-eyed stare. "She's no doubt been doing indecent things with him and feels bound to protect him."

"Miss Foote." Keely had squelched the urge to pull the cloche hat down over the woman's accusing eyes. "What is indecent is your assumption about Jed and about me." Keely had thought her statement was fairly mild considering what she'd really wanted to say.

Virginia Foote, however, had sat ruler-straight in the folding chair, her pump-clad feet a mere three inches from the hem of her gray linen dress, knees together, hands rigid on the closure of her roomy purse, and her face laced up in a whipstitch of wrinkles. Her cloche hat seemed friendly in comparison.

"Proper women do not carry weapons," she said pompously.

Keely had had nowhere to go with that comment except deeper into trouble. Judge Nelson had intervened then and told Keely she would have plenty of opportunity to present her side at the inquiry.

Keely and April had gone back to the cabin to pack their things. Keely insisted that April come home with her, and since Barbara had left her in Keely's care, the board had no authority to prevent it. The main objector had been Ellen Rivera, who regarded Keely as a glitch in what otherwise, as Ellen informed the board, would have been a flawless program.

That was two days ago. Today was day 30. Tonight, she thought disappointedly, her emotions raw from dwelling on the fact, would have been hers and Jed's. If he'd wanted her, he would have gotten in touch with her, but he hadn't. He hadn't come to see her, neither had he called.

April hung up the telephone and fiddled with the cord, her shoulders drooping. "She says she missed me."

Keely threw the remains of their lunch in the trash. "I'm sure she did. Let's get your things into the car and I'll take you home."

She straightened up. "Nothing has changed. Nothing."

Keely's nerves felt ragged. Whether it was the need to be by herself, or just weariness from trying to solve everyone else's problems, she wasn't sure. She didn't feel patient and understanding.

April had made no secret of not wanting to go home, or more specifically, not wanting to go home to a mother more interested in her boyfriend than in her daughter. Keely had told April numerous times that the problems she had with her mother were going to take longer than a two-week separation to work out. But they had to begin somewhere.

"Of course, something has changed. Bruce isn't just your mother's boyfriend any longer. She told me they're going to be married."

"And where does that leave me?"

"Exactly where you choose to be." Keely softened her voice. "April, your mother isn't perfect, but neither are you. You and she have been separated for two weeks. She sounded to me like she wanted to make a fresh start with you. Why don't you give her that chance?"

"And what if it doesn't work?" she asked belligerently.

"What if it does?"

Keely waited, watching the girl's head come up, her blue eyes widen. She sniffled, still winding the phone cord around her finger.

Then as though offering an olive branch, she murmured, "She said she wants me to be the maid of honor. Do you think she's just trying to make me feel wanted?"

Keely felt as if a large weight had fallen away. "You are wanted," she said, feeling a sudden warming toward Barbara. "The maid of honor is usually the bride's best friend. I think the next step is up to you."

The ride to April's house was silent, but more thoughtful on April's part than moody. When they arrived, Barbara came out to meet them. To Keely's relief, and April's surprise, Barbara looked like a mother who had honestly missed her daughter.

The reunion hug was tentative, the words somewhat awkward, but there was a hug and words. A start.

As Keely drove back to the beach house, she found her thoughts returning to Jed, her emotions on the verge of coming apart. Easily, she could blame the board or Turk and Snakeman. Easily, and rightly so, she could lay all the blame on her own foolish idea of invincibility when she brought April to the Island. But the what-ifs, and the regrets that she hadn't foreseen the disaster, were all hindsight at its depressing worst.

And, she thought, as she turned into the small driveway beside the beach house, it would be easy to allow herself to get very depressed. Perhaps that was what she should do. Wallow in self-pity, cry, get angry. Release all the bottled-up tension. For the two days that April had been with her, she'd held herself rigidly in check, crying only once during a lone run on the beach.

Keely closed the kitchen door, glad for the sudden silence that settled around her like a shroud. She crossed to the calendar, studied the two days not crossed off and then yanked the calendar off the wall. She tore it in half, then flung the pieces in the direction of the trash can. She swore, then slid down the wall landing on the floor with a plunk.

She sniffled, and raised her knees to her chin. Don't cry, she told herself. It was dumb to cry over a man. Wasn't there some saying about not worrying about losing one because another one always came along?

Except she didn't want another one. She wanted Jed. Maybe she should go to his apartment, plant herself in the middle of his bed and tell him she loved him.

Pride stopped her. Dumb female pride that told her she wasn't going to chase a man who didn't want her.

He wins. She loses. It was a lousy way to face the future. With her arms folded on top of her upraised knees, Keely lowered her head and cried.

It was after nine that evening when Keely ran the final lap between the lifeguard stand and the path that led back to the beach house. At last she stood on the shoreline, her toes working deep into the wet sand as the ocean flowed in and ebbed back out. Since the crying jag in the kitchen, she'd managed twelve whole seconds without thinking about Jed.

She should take a quick swim, she thought, but the water seemed cold and forbidding under the moonless night.

She stretched, cooled down now from her run.

Perhaps, she would get her hair cut, she thought with a toss of her braid over her shoulder. She walked up the path to the beach house. Something short and sassy. A new color, too. Blond. Hmm.

She halted a few feet from the deck, telling herself she must be seeing things, and at the same time praying she wasn't.

He was sitting on the railing, wearing those same faded-to-white jeans that had become so familiar to her those weeks on the Island. He wore no shirt. His back rested against the support beam, legs stretched out lazily, booted feet crossed at the ankles. In his hand was a soda. His leather jacket lay on the poppy-red-cushioned lounge.

"Jed." She breathed his name.

He absorbed her rather than saw her, allowing himself the luxury of obsessiveness. He took in everything about her, from her ocean-breeze-mussed hair, to her faded blue sweatshirt, to shorts he envied for their closeness to her body and finally to her sandy feet. He grinned at the way her toes burrowed into the sand. He could almost feel them riding up his naked calf.

His eyes came back to her face. She was mysteriously innocent and sexually fascinating. Dangerous, too, he knew, because Keely Lockwood penetrated his code of noncommitment. Take a woman, enjoy her, give her pleasure, but no surrender. It was a simple pattern that worked for him, that had always worked, that he was desperately afraid would not work with her.

Beyond heated kisses and his reaction to the depth of her response, Jed had wisely not allowed himself to indulge. And though he was the one who'd requested this one night, its potential unnerved him.

"You were all out of beer." His voice sounded rough.

"I hate beer." The answer was automatic, the scene a rerun of the last time he'd come to the beach house.

Except this time he wasn't crossing the deck to give her a chance to escape.

This time she wasn't naked.

This time she wished she was.

He raised the can to his mouth, drained it and let it drop into the sand. The beach grass barely moved. The lights from the house threw shadows.

The citronella candles should be lit, Keely thought with the minuscule part of her that wasn't coveting the sumptuous spread of dark hair that fanned across his chest.

How could he look both profane and prodigious in grubby jeans? Intimate places worn white taunted her gaze. She tried to count buttons and discovered her fingers tingled with expectation. Her feet felt mired in the sand.

From the light of the deck where he waited, to the shadows where she stood, desire whispered.

"Come here."

She swallowed, but nothing slid down her throat but dry heat. She tried to steady her breathing, feeling more winded than she did after a hard run.

He liked her reluctance. Her hesitation to rush forward. Her sudden shyness with him. "You didn't swim tonight."

He shifted with a slow grace that, to Keely, demonstrated the control she'd come to know so well. His thighs straddled the railing.

Four—no, five buttons. Knowing how many suddenly became vividly important. Her fingers filled with urgency. Straining denim. Heavy and rough in her palm.

Yes . . . oh, yes . . . She fantasized. Hot and wonderful. Her gaze blurred and she felt punch-drunk.

She replied, hoping she sounded sober and sane. "You told me it was dangerous to swim alone at night."

His palms rested on his thighs, hands very still, fingers spread very wide. "I wanted to see you come over the sand wet and naked."

"The last time—"

"The last time I wanted to devour you."

Keely thought her heart had stopped. He had noticed. He had! "This time you're more controlled."

"Barely, but this time I was prepared."

"I'm sorry you're disappointed."

"Not disappointed," he said with a huskiness that crept down her spine in a delicious tingle. "Never disappointed in anything about you."

Words she didn't expect. Words that kept her sumptuously off balance as Jed had done since she'd met him. A new joy, immense and dazzling, filled her soul. "You mean that, don't you?"

"Yes."

His eyes didn't mock or tease or drift away. Keely found herself more affected by the simple word, thick with truth and honesty, than any flowery compliment he could have given her.

"Are you going to walk over here so I can kiss you?"

She felt foolishly like Cinderella stepping forward to dance with the Prince. Carefully, she moved up onto the deck, her feet finding their footing, yet she felt as though she were walking on fluffy clouds.

"I thought you weren't going to come," she murmured.

He watched her mouth, liking the way she formed words, aroused by the delicate corners she moistened with her tongue.

He considered possible ways he could answer, knowing she hadn't realized the double meaning in her words. "I never intended not to come."

"But when I didn't hear from you ..." Her voice trailed off but she said silently, I was afraid you didn't want me.

"I wanted to wait until April was gone." Seeing you, and not making love to you, babe, would have killed me, he added silently.

"You knew she was here?"

"I talked to Seth. He told me."

She gulped.

She sought his eyes and discovered desire. Naked. Raw. Primitive. "I want you to do everything. I want to do everything to you."

She was coming closer to him now, and her scent seemed to fill the summer night. She touched the scar on his belly, tracing her finger slowly along the faded ridge, and then lowered her head. She brushed her mouth over the puckery flesh.

Wanting her tongue, Jed tangled one hand in her braid, his breathing harsh. "Ah, babe ... babe ..."

And when she licked his skin, at first tentatively, then boldly, he sucked in his breath. His control was crippled by the wetness of her touch.

She lifted her head, glancing at him, her eyes so green, so deep. He cupped the back of her neck, rubbing his mouth across lips he could no longer resist. Then his hands eased around her waist, lifting her so she, too, straddled the railing, facing him. He settled her thighs over his, and then adjusted her bottom so that she was pressed tightly and intimately against him.

He urged her head back, his hand once again winding around her braid. She laid her hands on the soft beating heat of his chest. Her mouth opened in greedy need, and Jed offered fulfillment. His tongue explored with a slow languorous sweep; he angled his head to move deeper, to drink sustenance to make up for every barren moment he'd been away from her.

Keely felt like a woman deprived of the touches and tastes of sensual pleasure. She whimpered when his hand prowled beneath her sweatshirt.

"You make me hot for you, babe. So hot," he murmured against her mouth. His hands burned along her ribs, not yet touching her breasts, making her want to cry out in frustration.

Once again his mouth settled on hers with a familiarity that was coated with desire. He explored her as if searching for some untapped passion.

Tongues tangled, thirsting for more. Tastes blended sweetly. Soft feminine arms wound tight and eager around a strong male neck. Callused hands explored curves, pressing hotly against waiting satin skin. Licking flames spread through their bodies, flames that scorched and seduced. Flames that promised a coming surrender.

Jed lifted his mouth, staring at her, at the moistness his kiss had left on her lips. "I think I just discovered sex."

She grinned, her eyes sparkling with life and desire.

"We're going to be good together, aren't we?"

Jed kissed her again. "If I don't die before we get to the bedroom."

He pulled her sweatshirt off, tossing it aside, stopping when he saw her bra.

"It's for running," she whispered.

"It looks virginal."

"It's made for support, not to look sexy."

His hand fanned her back, searching. "No hooks."

"It's spandex." She tried to slide back from him, so she could pull off the bra, but he stopped her. He seemed fascinated with its elasticity and with exploring her breasts through it.

"Doesn't it hurt you, being all bound up like that?"

"Not usually."

"Not usually?"

"I'm not usually aroused when I wear it."

His eyes slowly closed, and the words he uttered were explicit and raw. Keely treasured them all.

Carefully he pulled the bra over her head to reveal breasts that were delicately shaped, and nipples a deep rose color. They pearled eagerly when his hands closed over first one breast and then the other. His thumbs eased over the peaks. They were so delicate, like gossamer. Keely's breathing shallowed.

His fingers settled at her waist, and he lifted her slightly. Then he lowered his head, his mouth taking first one nipple and then the other in a sucking motion that made her gasp. Threading her fingers through his hair, she pressed him to her. She arched back, languishing in the sweet pleasure.

Jed spread his hand over her lower back, his fingers sliding under the elastic of her running shorts. Kissing each nipple, lingering to savor its texture one more time, he lifted her off him and set her on the deck. Keely staggered, but he was there swinging her up and into his arms.

She snuggled her head into his neck, pressing wet kisses there. "Hurry, Jed," she murmured.

In her bedroom he put her down, steadying her. The light from a small lamp kissed the darkness with a soft glow. Jed drew her back into his arms. "I can't stop touching you," he muttered against her hair.

"I want to unbutton you," she whispered. When her hands fluttered over his skin, skimming down the buttons, feathering the hard denim, then sliding back up and finally getting the first opened, Jed knew he'd never last through the second one, never mind the last.

"Better let me do it, babe." The rest of the buttons opened reluctantly. Keely watched him. No man had ever been so beautifully made. Lean and hard. Aroused. She caught his hips when the last button was opened. They faced each other, both bare to the waist, both desperate, both trying to draw out each precious moment.

He drew her hands around and put them inside his jeans, dragging air into his lungs when she touched him. Her knees sagged and he caught her, his own control completely lost. He lifted her so that her legs wrapped around him, and with his own legs apart to balance them, he rocked her.

She blew a puff of air across his mouth.

He caught it and kissed her.

"We got a problem," he murmured, finding the skin below her ear delicate and warm—a sensual discovery.

"I know." She pressed the black silk of his hair against her cheek, wiggling her hips closer to him. "We're still half-dressed."

"This usually works better without clothes."

"Hmmm, okay." She'd found that by her rocking just a little to the side, his breathing became twice as fast.

He walked the few steps to the bed and lowered them both, his body covering hers. He kissed her again, rubbed his cheek on her breasts and then lifted himself off her long enough to get out of his jeans and boots.

Her eyes never leaving him, Keely wiggled out of her shorts.

Jed stood still and stared.

She wore white cotton panties. Not silk or nylon or some lacy nothing, but plain white cotton. It both amazed and excited him that he found them incredibly sexy. They were cut high on her legs, with the sides tantalizingly bare. He traced the elastic band, his fingers insinuating themselves under the cotton.

"I've never made love to a woman who wears white cotton panties," he whispered as he pulled them off.

"I've never made love to a man who doesn't wear underwear," she whispered back. "That makes us special."

"Yes, very special." Leaning over her, he touched her stomach with his hand, and then so slowly that Keely thought a century passed, he drew his palm down until it rested in the warmth between her thighs.

She caught her breath when he kissed the dewy curls. "Oh . . ." It was too delicate, and she raised her hips, wanting more.

She felt him smile. "Even here you smell like violets," he murmured, and kissed her again.

His mouth touched her stomach, her breasts, the trembling pulse in her throat, and finally her lips. She brushed her fingers up his thigh; his skin felt crinkly with hair that softened as her hand came closer to his sex.

He groaned when she curled her fingers around him. For long seconds their breaths stopped while she explored. Reluctantly, he lifted her hand away. Kissing her deeply, he rolled off her and reached for his jeans.

"Jed?" Her arms flailed, trying to find him, trying to pull him back.

"I'm not leaving, babe."

In the soft light, she saw him pull a foil packet out of his pocket. Protection, she thought. Always, he wants to protect me. She loved him for that, but she wanted nothing between them.

He came down beside her, his knee nudging her thighs wider. As she pulled him on top of her, he stared down at her, at the dazzle of arousal and eagerness in her eyes. It came to him not as a flash of insight, but as a long-buried hope that with Keely Lockwood...

Hope got lost in need. He kissed her. He covered her. He settled against her as though he'd come home, as though tomorrow and forever were caught in this moment.

She lifted her hips, wiggling and drawing him deep into her, wishing the soft protective sheath didn't separate them.

Jed groaned, the desire for completion rushing within him. He'd waited too long. He'd wanted her too much.

She didn't hold back; her body shivered and arched.

She cried out, her legs coming up, gripping him tighter.

And at the moment of her pleasure, when she was straining against him, he felt her tears against his neck.

She wanted to cry out that she loved him, that she'd love him forever. She wanted to cry, don't leave me.

He felt her peak. Their bodies were in erotic suspension.

"Oh, God," he groaned raggedly when she called his name with a breathless shudder at the crest of fulfillment.

*   *   *

The night was too short, the lovemaking too greedy, too compelling, too satiating. Keely refused to acknowledge the emptiness of afterward. Jed dreaded it.

At five o'clock he lay awake, watching the new day emerge on the horizon. Her body was half-sprawled over him; her legs were tangled with his. Her breathing was deep, the rhythm even.

The second time, he'd unbraided her hair and spread it across his belly, rubbing it against his skin as he watched her mouth move lower.

The third time she'd ridden him. Hard. Wild.

After the fourth time he'd run out of foil packets.

"Hell," he'd muttered when he realized there were no more. The small clock read 3:12 a.m. Too late for any drugstore to be open. He dropped his jeans back on the floor.

"I hate them," she said from behind him. She wrapped her arms around his middle, kissing his back. "I'm glad you finally ran out."

He was angry that he hadn't brought six dozen, frustrated because he was nowhere near satisfied, scared because when her hands moved over his sex, he didn't give a damn about protection or control.

He gripped her wrists, his voice brittle. "You sure won't like being knocked up."

If he thought that would discourage her, he quickly found out differently. "How do you know? Maybe I would."

"Keely, for God's sake."

"You said there'd be no afterward," she said on the edge of tears. "I want you. I want all I can get while I have you. Jed, at least give me that."

"And what if you get pregnant?"

He'd turned and was staring at her, his question an echo in the tense air.

She closed her eyes for a long second, and when her lashes fluttered open again, she met his gaze with a bald honesty that made him question and wonder and, yes, hope.

"I don't think I'll be that lucky," she whispered, her green eyes suddenly shiny with tears.

His control snapped. He swore, taking her down onto the bed, finding her and entering her and loving the unsheathed softness of her. Her heat. Her words. Her unquenchable need.

Just thinking back on it now, and the two more times that had followed, made him stir with a renewed desire. He knew he'd made her sore, and hated himself for still wanting her.

Slowly, he untangled himself from her, feeling as if he were letting go of a lifeline. To leave while she was asleep was a coward's way out, but he couldn't face her.

Walking around the bed, he pulled on his jeans and closed only the bottom three buttons. She stirred and he froze.

"Jed?" She sounded sleepy and sexy.

He smoothed her hair back, pressing his knuckles against her warm cheek, wanting to soak up the feel and smell of her. "Shh, go back to sleep, babe."

She murmured something, her voice fuzzy in the early light of dawn. He kissed her then, softly, and her arms came up to close around his neck and draw him to her. He knew her mouth was greedy for deeper kisses, more intimate touches. "Are we going to make love again?"

"In a little while," he whispered. Liar. Liar.

She snuggled down, a smile appearing on her mouth. Contentment filled him at what he wanted to believe was a smile of deep satisfaction.

He kissed her once again. Her mouth. Her breasts. The dewy curls. He inhaled the violets. At 5:25, he covered her with the blue summer quilt.

When her phone rang at ten o'clock, Keely, pleasantly sore and groggy but satisfied, struggled out of the covers to answer it. Judge Nelson told her the board's inquiry was scheduled for Friday of the following week.

"I can't get any answer at Corey's," he told Keely sharply. "He needs to be notified. Is there any chance you can get in touch with him?"

She grinned sleepily, rolling onto her back and then turning toward the middle of the bed where she'd last loved him.

Cold sheets and only a bare trace of his scent greeted her.

Chapter 12

Jed couldn't remember the last time he'd been down-and-dirty drunk.

And not on beer. She hated beer, he reminded himself as he stumbled across his apartment to his unmade bed. This was the hard stuff. Good stuff. Jack Daniel's. Premium. A smooth, easy-going-down drunk.

He broke the seal on the third bottle, his hands amazingly steady. He didn't feel anything but a vague pain that didn't want to ease.

For more than a week, he'd been working on the ache, on forgetting the long braid and the spring-green eyes. On forgetting she had a soft spot for hurt creatures.

He tossed the bottle cap out the open window.

Rain splashed inside, soaking the curtains and dripping off the sill. On the floor under the window lay a pile of methodically torn paper, only hours old, but already a soggy mess.

He sprawled on his bed, unbuttoned jeans barely on his hips. No boots. No shirt. Unshaved. He hoisted the bottle and toasted the damp chilly room.

"To you, Ma, wherever you are. Your kid finally made it. The kid you didn't want. The kid no one wanted. He screwed up like you said he would. Turned out like his old man, whoever he was. A heartless no-good drunken bastard." He took a long pull and swallowed the liquid, trying to burn away her taste.

His apartment door eased open. A leery Oakes peered inside and muttered with disgust. "Hell, Jed, not another bottle."

Grinning, Jed reached down beside the bed, lifted two more unopened ones to show his landlord and then dropped them. One tipped over and rolled under the bed. He stopped smiling. "Shut the door on your way out."

Oakes shook his head. "You got to get up, man, and get yourself sober."

Jed frowned, trying to clear his blurry mind. He'd tried to deal with "the afterward" by working days and drinking himself to sleep at night. But the sober days, despite the hard work, were too clogged with thoughts of her. Drinking steadily now for two days should have been enough to drown the most stubborn memory. Yet he couldn't shake her.

He'd spent only one night with her. One night that was supposed to satisfy him, but instead it left him edgy and empty. "What day is it?"

"Friday. That inquiry is in a few hours."

He lifted the bottle. "Heartless drunken bastards need not apply. Go away."

Oakes shuffled inside and closed the door. He shifted his cigar stub to the other side of his mouth. "Drunk, yeah. Heartless, no."

"But a bastard. Know what a bastard is?" He raised and wiggled two fingers in front of his mouth. "Shh. No old man. A secret, so secret the old lady didn't catch his name. Shh . . ."

Oakes shook his head again when he saw the mess under the window. "Come on, Jed, let me call someone. What about the Judge's daughter?"

Jed narrowed his eyes. "No."

"She's got somethin' to do with all this, don't she?" he asked with a bitterness Jed heard even through the bleary fog of Jack Daniel's. Uptown bitches with a hot city itch, Oakes called them. "I coulda swore she was an okay broad, but lookin' at you—damn! I've known you too long and I've never seen you this messed up."

"Control, Mugsy, my man," he said on a loud belch. He followed with another drink from the bottle. "Control."

"And you're still controlled. That's the problem."

"I'm dealin' with the problem here, Mugsy. I'm findin' what I lost with her. Control—yep. That's it. I'll get it back." He raised the bottle, squinting at the liquor level.

"Jed, you might be a sloshed, unshaved slob and not able to get your butt off the bed, but the control is still there. If you'd lost it, you'd be with her. She got to you, didn't she?"

He frowned, staring at the amber liquid, cursing it for not letting him forget her. "Knock off the shrink stuff. I don't want to talk about her."

Mugsy grinned. Wider. And wider still. "I'll be . . . She did get to you."

Jed glared and saw three of him. "Shut up."

"What's wrong with that? The great, never-let-himself-love-a-woman finally met his match in Keely Lockwood. I know you're scared it won't work, but man, life ain't got no guarantees. You love her, doncha?"

Jed looked at him too long. He wanted her. He wanted to forget her. He wanted to get back into the nice safe world of controlled feelings and emotions. There was no pain there. No disappointment. No rejection. "Bull. You see her around here? Do I look like a guy in love, whatever that is?"

"You look like a guy scared right down to his socks, in your case, your bare feet."

Jack Daniel's was supposed to make her go away, make the pain of wanting her go away. Jack, do your stuff. Jed hoisted the bottle once more.

The inquiry room was in the same building as Judge Nelson's courtroom. Barren of warmth or personality, it waited with no welcome, but no condemnation, either. Some nicks marred the sand beige walls the chairs had been pushed back against. The windows were naked and sealed out the fresh air. Central air droned. The rain lashed at the glass; the sky was sunless, the heavy clouds stained gray, their movement across the heavens slow.

A long conference table occupied the middle of the room. A dozen or so chairs were scattered around it as if a sudden fire drill had sent everyone scurrying out the door. Ashtrays were on the table, and a lone ballpoint pen. In one corner, in a garden-green plastic pot, an overstressed plant stretched for the window light as well as a drink of water.

Keely occupied a chair by the plant.

She'd arrived early deliberately. She didn't want to make any kind of entrance, and she wanted to be prepared for each one who came in.

She reached up to flip her braid over her shoulder and found nothing. Would he recognize her with the short haircut?

Her mother almost hadn't. Rosemary Lockwood had been out of town visiting friends. On her return, a few days ago, she'd stopped to see Keely.

"My God, what did you do to your hair?"

"I had it cut."

"But it was so pretty, long and—"

"I wanted a change."

"Darling, tell me what's wrong. I know things didn't go well on the Island, but this isn't like you."

So she told her mother, and after she finished, they simply sat together quietly. There was nothing more to say.

Would he recognize her with the short haircut? Then she wondered if he'd even bother to look at her.

She wore a navy-blue suit and a prim white blouse buttoned to the neck. His mark lay under the blouse on the top of her left breast. Her palm located it without her glancing down, and she pressed it, held it. It matched the one on the inside of her right thigh. That was almost gone now, fading with time, as other things did. She'd searched for the marks this morning with a frantic terror that convinced her she must be teetering on the edge of madness.

Any day now she should be able to put it all behind her. Him, his touch, his buttoned jeans and no underwear. His surprising way of always keeping her off balance. His fierce protective attitude. She never had found out about the scrapbook, one of the first things she'd found different about him. One of the last things she'd never know about him.

Ten days had passed. Or had it been ten lifetimes?

That morning, when she'd turned over and found him gone, she'd known it was over. She'd tried to tell herself it wasn't over, but she'd known. He'd left no note, and he hadn't called her later to say he'd changed his mind. She'd even run the beach for five nights, hoping to come up the sandy path and find him waiting on the deck. But he didn't come. He hadn't been kidding. He'd meant it when he said there'd be no afterward.

Since Monday, when she'd had her hair cut, she'd functioned between numbing tears and a cold acceptance of reality. A voice inside her whispered that real love didn't give up, didn't resign itself to a barren future alone; that real love would fight the way she'd fought to get the directorship at Black Horse.

Real love would fight for Jed.

Both, logic told her, were now impossibilities.

She couldn't blame him. Blame belonged to deception. He'd never tried to deceive her. He hadn't lied to her. He'd made no promises, and he'd committed himself to nothing beyond one night.

Keely closed her eyes and squeezed her thighs together. The pleasure he'd given her still made her shiver. But as wonderful as those physical feelings were, they didn't compensate for the ravagement of her soul; for a cut so deep into her being, she knew it would never heal.

The first arrivals stood in the doorway.

"Hello, Seth, Irma," she said, hoping she sounded sane and not like a zombie.

"Keely-kid, is that you?" Seth responded. "What did you do to your hair? Are you okay? You look like you've lost weight."

He appeared uncomfortable in his brown suit. His red-and-blue tie was slightly askew, and it pulled on his white shirt collar as though one or the other didn't fit. His gray hair was sprinkled with raindrops.

Irma stood beside him wearing a polyester dress. Her hair had a fresh blue rinse, her eyes were unintrusive and warm. To Keely the combination made her seem like a grandmother. She carried a plastic raincoat and rain bonnet. Her paisley umbrella dripped water onto the gray carpet making dark gray spots.

"Seth," Irma said, giving his arm a shake, "you only say that to women who need to lose weight. Like me."

He smiled down at her. "I like you the way you are."

"You better. I'm too old for all that dieting stuff."

"Can I ask her why she cut off all her hair?" he asked, like a little boy wanting permission.

Irma peered at Keely, obviously as interested as Seth.

Keely answered them. "I got tired of braiding it every morning."

Seth rubbed his chin. "But it makes you look gaunt and underfed, don't you think, Irma?"

"That's because we're used to seeing it long. I think it's lovely because Keely is a lovely sweet girl."

Keely smiled and whispered a soft thank-you for what she knew was a sincere compliment from Irma. Lovely sweet girl, however, sounded like April. She liked Jed's description. Sensational had a lushness that made her feel sexy.

Seth and Irma stood together staring at her for a few moments. Then he cleared his throat and guided Irma over to a group of chairs. "We supposed to sit anywhere special?'' he asked no one in particular. ''We never had to come to one of these when the Judge ran the Island. Here, sit here, Irma.''

Keely laced her hands together and squeezed. She knew Seth too well to believe his comment was some low-blow shot, yet it was true. When her father was director, an inquiry would have never been necessary.

She thought of dreams and fulfilling dreams, of making her father proud of her. None of that mattered. Her father was gone. The dream was a web of energy she'd substituted for the truth. Had her father preferred the Island to his family? Had he loved kids like Jed more than his own daughter? Those were the questions. After all that had happened she still didn't know the answers.

The board members arrived.

Dr. Lewis with his notebook.

John McGovern, the former governor, with his concerned smile that Keely decided came very close to pity.

Ellen Rivera, the frown lines in her brow now etched into a look of despondency, making Keely feel like a one-woman disaster team.

Judge Nelson, brisk looking in a pressed blue suit, with a fresh haircut and wafting the scent of expensive after-shave.

Virginia Foote in her hat, her mouth compressed so tight that a kind word couldn't escape even if it were escorted out by an angel.

Keely nodded to each one as they entered. Not smiling, but feeling somewhat as if she'd been waiting for the return of a jury to declare her guilty.

Judge Nelson sat at the head of the table. ''Who are we missing?''

"That Corey person," Virginia Foote said as if he had a communicable disease and she had neglected to get inoculated. She adjusted her hat, taking the chair closest to the judge.

"Did you get in touch with him, Keely?" He scowled at her, looking puzzled rather than impatient. "You look different. You're not sick, are you?"

"I'm fine," she said after clearing her throat. "I talked to his landlord. He said he'd give him the message."

"He's late," Ellen announced, making *late* sound like a first-degree murder charge.

"There is no reason to wait for him," Keely said. "Jed did exactly what he was supposed to do on the Island. Any questions you have I can answer."

Virginia Foote stiffened. Beneath the jut of her chin, Keely saw a pea-sized mole. "That, Ms. Lockwood, is a matter to be decided by this board."

Dr. Lewis scribbled furiously. Judge Nelson scowled again. Irma scooted her chair closer to Seth.

The judge opened a folder and took out a piece of flower-decorated stationery. "I have a letter here from Mrs. Solitto. By the way, we talked to the kids earlier in the week. They had quite a few interesting things to say about you and Corey."

None of them revealed anything in their faces. Keely wondered if there was some official course offered to potential board members on how to look bland and blank.

"How are the kids? And Turk? He'd come so far until—" She bit her lip and kept her eyes wide open. She had to keep herself from sinking deeper in the quagmire of guilt. If she hadn't brought the switchblade. If she hadn't brought April.

"Mrs. Solitto is very pleased with the change in her son. Apparently, he's sent word to the court that he wants to work on that volunteer housing project for low-income families that's been going on for the past year or so, the one Corey is involved in. Turk's mother requested to come today to thank you personally, Keely, but one of her children is sick."

Keely thought of the house Turk and the other kids had built for the generator. It had been Jed's project to teach them a skill. "I'm glad for Turk. What are the chances the court will let him do it?"

"They'll probably allow it for a probationary period." Then glancing at Seth, Judge Nelson said, "Would you go and call to find out where Corey is."

Then the judge looked toward the opening door, as did everyone else.

Keely sucked in her breath and had to force herself not to react in any way. He was wearing a dark suit, and her first thought was that it didn't belong to him. It was too big, and looked as out of place on him as a fedora and a gold pocket watch would have. His hair was shaggy and wet from the rain. Sunglasses covered his eyes, and Keely saw his walk lacked its usual smoothness, although to the casual observer it would have seemed steady.

If it hadn't been for the slightly gray cast to his cheeks and the obvious shaving cut on his chin, Keely told herself she wouldn't have stared so hard.

He made his way to the nearest chair.

She watched him without blinking, remembering his silky hair on her breasts, the sweep of his tongue in her mouth. His words...

I can't stop touching you...

I've never made love to a woman who wears white cotton panties . . .

Even here you smell like violets . . .

Keely dug her fists into her lap.

"Corey, sit over there with the others," the judge said.

Jed seemed to consider arguing, but said nothing. Slowly he walked toward her. Her heart began to thump, and the room seemed to run out of oxygen.

Seth stood up and moved to another chair. "Sit here, Jed. You should be beside Keely," he said in a low voice.

With a chilled hand, Keely steadied the chair, for no reason other than that as he got closer she realized he wasn't completely sober.

She wished she could see his eyes. His condition gave her hope, only because he wasn't as controlled. No, his control had most assuredly suffered a major blow. She decided he looked terrible. She decided he looked sensational.

Gingerly he lowered himself into the chair.

"Want some coffee?" she whispered, not sure she'd be allowed to leave to get him some. But she was interested in hearing him say something.

He angled his head slightly, slowly, and she sensed he was doubtful it would stay on his shoulders. The glasses remained over his eyes. Suddenly Keely was very conscious of the way he looked naked and aroused.

"What in hell did you do to your hair?" His voice was ragged and raw as if he hadn't used it much.

"You're sober enough to notice?"

"I don't like it."

Suddenly, she felt a burst of anger. After the way he'd left her, he had no right to have any opinion about her. "I don't recall asking you if you liked it."

His hand slid down the dark suit and paused in the general area of his stomach. She wondered if he was recalling the way he'd dragged her hair across him, or if he felt nauseated.

She saw him frown and set his mouth in a tight grimace. Then he nodded in the direction of the board members. "Sorry I'm late," he mumbled, folding his arms as if the gesture would keep him upright. Keely refolded her hands in her lap. She wasn't sorry she'd cut her hair. She wasn't. She couldn't bear to brush it every morning, knowing how it had felt tangled in his fists.

Virginia Foote sniffed, her head bobbing and dipping. "Do I detect an odor of spirits?" she asked like a teetotaler.

Judge Nelson patted her hand. "You're imagining things."

Dr. Lewis and Ellen Rivera joined in the sniffing.

"Didn't notice it before," Dr. Lewis said, his pen poised over his notebook, his attention on Jed.

Keely glanced at Jed. He'd slouched farther down in the chair, and she heard him curse. Their thighs brushed, and the jolt zigzagged up to settle in her womb. Jed jerked his leg away. She wanted to think he was as affected by her as she was by him, but she didn't want to fool herself. She looked back at Virginia Foote, and managed an embarrassed laugh. "I'm afraid I'm responsible."

Every eye in the room zeroed in on her.

Jed went very still beside her. She didn't dare look at him. She cleared her throat. "Someone left a small flask of whiskey in this poor plant. I picked it up to throw it away and I spilled it.''

Everyone continued to look at her, then at the wilting plant as if it might confirm her story or at least die a drunken death. Only Jed didn't look at the plant. He stared at her. She felt his eyes even through the sunglasses.

''Spirits are *not* allowed in here, Ms. Lockwood,'' Virginia Foote said. Her cloche hat drooped lower.

''And that's why I got rid of it, Miss Foote,'' Keely replied in her best fifth-grade voice.

She saw the amused smile on both Judge Nelson's and John McGovern's faces. Dr. Lewis turned the page of his notebook. Irma told Seth to close his mouth.

While the board members put their heads together as to how to proceed, and Seth asked Irma to tell him what he missed, Jed leaned sideways. Keely leaned, too.

Their shoulders brushed. Their thighs touched again. This time neither moved away. He felt solid and warm, and she wondered if he still had the mark she'd left on his thigh.

''I don't need you to rescue me,'' he growled out of the side of his mouth.

''I'm paying you back.''

''For what?''

''For the lie you told about owning the switchblade. Now we're both liars.'' She smiled at him. ''And Miss Foote is right. There is a distinct odor of spirits.''

His mouth twitched into a near grin, and Keely's heart skittered. ''Jack Daniel's.''

She grinned a tiny grin back. ''Does it make the hangover any better?''

''It makes getting drunk smoother.''

"You should have called me. I would have joined you."

"You!" Glancing at the others, he lowered his voice to a hoarse whisper. "You don't even like beer."

"You are in bad shape. Don't you remember I like whiskey?"

He scowled.

She dropped her voice to a hush. "And I love you."

The foot he'd been trying to balance on his knee dropped to the floor with a loud thud. His body slid forward and Keely grabbed his jacket sleeve to keep him in the chair.

She felt a little jump of encouragement at his reaction. She'd surprised herself, too, by allowing the words to slide out like an unanticipated gift. She'd thought them, relished them, but had never said them. The room wasn't exactly a romantic setting; neither was the darkening scowl on his face very romantic.

"Let's proceed," Judge Nelson said. "Keely, since I have this glowing letter from Turk's mother, tell us about his behavior on the Island."

Keely began. For the next two hours, she answered questions. Then Jed answered questions. Finally they came to the issue of April.

Judge Nelson gathered up the folders, closed them and glanced at each board member. "The issue of the Isherwood girl is important because she was there without authorization." He regarded Keely with a stern look. "Am I to assume that when you were here to give me the preliminary reports, April was not at the Island?"

"She wasn't. It happened after I left here." Keely gave as many details as she could remember. She knew that the board's decision would rest on whether or not they accepted her reasons for taking April to the Island.

Jed sat up. "Can I say something?"

Judge Nelson nodded.

Jed started to get to his feet, thought better of it and settled for leaning forward. He gave Keely a long intense look, and then centered his attention on the waiting listeners. "As important as rules are, there are times when they need to be broken. When Turk went after Snakeman with the knife, it was to protect April. You may not agree with that, but there was more at stake than a couple of kids having a fight. Turk knew he would be in trouble for having the knife. Gutting someone would get him tossed off the Island."

Virginia Foote and Dr. Lewis both turned a pale gray.

Jed took a breath, and Keely wanted to slip her hand through his arm. "He chose to risk that to save April."

"Now, when Keely brought April to the Island, she got a long lecture from me and from Seth about the dangerous situation a pretty girl would create. Both of us wanted April sent back to the mainland. Keely, like Turk, was more interested in the girl and what she needed than in what the rules said."

Ellen Rivera folded her hands, her voice textbook perfect. "That's all very interesting. However, if the rules had been followed— Incidentally, Judge Lockwood always did follow the rules and without exception." She aimed a look at Keely. "As I recall, he didn't allow even his family on the Island, he was so conscious of the volatility of mixing the sexes. If the Isherwood girl had been placed with a social worker, as she should have been, none of this would have happened. Correct?"

"And she'd be a runaway," Keely said. "Is that what the system wants? Follow the rules, but lose the kids?"

"It is hardly the fault of the system that the girl's mother chose to leave her daughter vulnerable to those boys," Ellen responded.

"No, it isn't," Jed said, his voice sharp, angry. "But it sure as hell isn't Keely's, either."

The intensity behind his words made her think of principles and honor—and his never-changing need to protect her. Despite everything, that hadn't changed.

He stood up, remarkably steady on his feet. "She did what her father would have done. No, correction. She did more than her father would have done. She put her future and her dreams on the line for one young girl who needed her."

Jed's words impressed the board. Even Virginia Foote allowed her face to soften. Once again they put their heads together, but Keely's mind wasn't on the decision they would make, pro or con. One comment Jed had made needed to be questioned.

Keeping her voice low, she asked, "What do you mean, *more* than Dad would have done?"

He took off the sunglasses, his eyes blinking at the sudden exposure to light. But before he could say anything, Judge Nelson called on Seth. The questions went on for another half hour. Dr. Lewis began a new notebook.

Finally, at 4:18 Judge Nelson made his concluding remarks. He specifically asked Keely to remain while he and the board retired to another area to agree on a position. They filed through a door Keely had thought led into a closet, but that turned out to lead to a smaller room.

"Are we to presume a verdict will be handed down?" Jed asked when the door closed. Seth said he was going to find some coffee. Irma excused herself to go to the ladies' room.

Jed got to his feet. "I think I'll go."

Keely grabbed his jacket sleeve. "Oh no, you won't."

"I won't?"

"I want to talk to you."

"That's what I was afraid of."

"Relax," she said, feeling the muscle tense beneath the fabric, seeing the throbbing in his temple. "I won't embarrass you by commenting on your deplorable condition. Or even why you're in that condition." She paused to see if he would say anything. He simply sagged back in the chair.

"What did you mean when you said I did more than Dad would have done?"

"Look, forget I said anything."

"You know something about my father I don't know. Don't you? Answer me, Jed."

He winced, his eyes closing and then opening. He peered at her. "You sure you aren't moonlighting as a prosecuting attorney?"

"Don't try to change the subject."

"Don't yell. Please. I've got a headache."

He winced again and this time she reached up and rubbed his neck. She felt him unexpectedly lean into her fingers.

"Don't stop," he muttered, rotating his head under her massaging fingers. Keely continued to knead in a slow rhythm. "There, right there," he said when, using both hands, she worked on his shoulders.

For a few minutes they didn't talk. She felt Jed slowly relax. Keeping her voice low, she said, "Look, maybe

I'm reading between the lines, but I had a very real feeling that Dad wouldn't have taken April over there."

Jed sighed. "I don't think he would have. He was adamant about not having girls on the Island."

"But Barbara Isherwood told me Dad planned to start a program for girls, and add extra staff to accommodate them."

Jed shook his head. "Only talk. He never would have done it. He told me that. He told me a month before he died."

She stopped massaging. "You were seeing Dad? On a regular basis?"

Jed shifted and tipped his head to the side. "On the back part of my shoulder. Yeah, there," he said when she moved her hands and began kneading again. "We met for breakfast at the diner a couple of times a month. The last year or so he'd been questioning whether to continue the Island program. Because of the red tape, the paperwork, and I think because he wanted to spend time with Rosemary and with you."

"It was too late. I needed him when I was sixteen." She said it too quickly and wanted to take it back. No, she decided. It was true. It was the way she felt. He hadn't been there when she needed him.

"Sometimes, I felt like I lived in a pretty box," she said softly, verbally expressing for the first time a pain she'd grown up feeling. Her hands stopped again, but stayed on his shoulders. "I only got attention on special occasions. It sounds so selfish when I say it out loud. And I guess I always felt guilty. He was doing so much good. I had everything a little girl could want."

"Except her father." He turned around and looked at her.

Her eyes were wide and vulnerable. "You do understand."

"Emotional poverty isn't limited to the ghetto, Keely. Look at April."

Look at you, she wanted to add. So afraid to feel, so afraid to hope and so very afraid to love. "Yes," she said with the smallest rasp to her voice. "But I think everything will work out for April."

"Thanks to you. I told you once your father would be proud of you for your effort to continue his dream. He'd be even prouder of your success."

"Some success. Unless the board decides in my favor, I'll be back doing paperwork in the city."

"You're not listening to me. You're seeing success as a big overall picture. It isn't. It's one young girl who chooses not to run away. It's a bully who comes to the defense of someone weaker. Don't you see?" He tipped her chin up, making her look at him, wanting her to understand. "You've had a profound and lasting influence on two young lives. That's a lot better than some misty dream."

Keely swallowed the sudden tightness in her throat. She let his words settle, pondering them, relating them to her own questions about her father.

She'd done the same thing with him. She was looking for some all-encompassing answer as to how he felt about her. Perhaps he hadn't been around as much as she would have liked. Perhaps he truly believed the kids like Jed needed him more than his family. Her father was human.

Jed had told her that day at his apartment that he wasn't some saint and he wasn't God. Her father hadn't been, either.

She allowed her eyes to close. Had her father preferred the Island to his family? Had he loved kids like Jed more than his own daughter? They were mammoth emotional questions, big-picture questions that were impossible to answer. She knew if her father were here now, and if she asked him directly, he would say no.

She looked up at Jed. He had fought his way through his emotionally and financially impoverished background. A life changed forever, she thought.

"Jed, if you hadn't gone through the program, what do you think would have happened?"

He'd crossed the room. He turned, giving her a strange look. "You're kidding. I owe everything to your father." ·

Gratitude, although Keely knew it was really love. Gratitude to her father, which in turn had led to protection of her. Both were traits her father had instilled in him. Traits that had drawn her to Jed and stirred her first feelings of love for him.

But Jed didn't want her.

He claimed to know nothing about love and commitment, but the reality was he was afraid of them with a woman.

Oh God. The truth rolled through her.

"Jed?"

But he was gone. She stood, moving quickly to the door, when Jedge Nelson emerged from the smaller room. The board filed out behind him.

"Sorry we took so long," Judge Nelson said. "Everyone but you decided not to wait, huh? Doesn't matter. Our decision concerns you."

Keely looked once more at the door, hoping Jed would reappear.

"We found in your favor."

"What?"

"You will remain as director, if that's what you want."

It was, wasn't it? She hadn't failed. The Island would continue, but she knew she wanted more. "What about Jed?"

Virginia Foote sniffed. "I don't approve of him. Nor do I like him, but the young man named Turk spoke of him as if he were, well, I hesitate even in conversation to compare that Corey person to the Almighty, but..."

"As if Jed was God," Keely added softly.

"Well," she said with a huff, "we all know the young man is wrong."

"Perhaps admiration and gratitude would be better words."

Ellen Rivera actually nodded in agreement. Dr. Lewis closed his notebook. John McGovern smiled.

Judge Nelson said, "The next group won't be sent over until September. Remind Corey that alcohol is forbidden, as are weapons, and from you, I'll need weekly reports."

Keely groaned. "I hate the paperwork."

"A necessity, Keely, if you're going to work with a state program."

Irma and Seth returned, and when they heard the news, they both eagerly embraced Keely.

"The Judge would be proud, Keely-kid," Seth said, "Yep, he sure would be proud."

Chapter 13

When she opened the door to his apartment, she found Jed had already changed his clothes. He stood by the window barefoot, wearing the familiar buttoned jeans and unbuttoned shirt. He was staring down at a soggy mess of paper under the window.

Keely slipped off her shoes, the wooden floor cold against her feet. "Why did you leave?"

He went very still for a moment. "I wanted to get out of the suit."

He glanced at her bare feet, and then back down at the mess. Keely saw the empty and the full bottles of Jack Daniel's on the card table. The bed was rumpled.

"I don't mean the inquiry. I mean ten mornings ago."

"To avoid the scene we're about ready to have."

"I love you," she whispered.

Jed stared at her. This time the words didn't startle him. Coming from her now, they sounded soft, almost innocent, almost real. Real. Don't fall for them, he told himself, every woman who'd ever said them to him could make them sound real. "Stop saying that," he snapped.

She halted her progress into the room, brushing the rain off her shoulders. She shivered slightly as the chilly wind blew in from the open window. "It's true," she said softly, not feeling as bold as she had at the inquiry.

"What you feel is only the result of good sex."

She shook her head.

He came across the room and took her by the shoulders. "No, strike good sex. Great sex. You were better than any woman I've ever had. I couldn't get enough of you. And right now, despite a hell of a headache, I could tumble you onto that bed and keep you there for the next month."

Her eyes were so green, so willing. "I wouldn't object."

He let go of her, almost pushing her away. "Go home, Keely. Get out of here."

Her next words scrambled out fast, as if she were desperate and afraid she'd lose her nerve. "What if I refuse to leave? What if I seduce you? What if I tell you all I want is you? No commitment. No marriage. You don't even have to worry about that emotion you say you don't know anything about." Then taking a deep breath, she lowered her head. "There could be lots of options in an afterward."

"Options like what?" he countered sharply. "Come on, you're the one with all the fast answers. You're the counselor. Let me have the options."

She swallowed. "Being together. Making love."

"Yeah? Go on. That will last about six months."

"How do you know?"

"Because I've been there. I've tried living with women. I've tried pretending they wanted nothing else but that. Not true. They want marriage and kids, and don't try to tell me you don't or won't later. I watched you with Turk and April and the rest. Babe, you're the most committed woman I've ever known."

"But you haven't even given us a chance."

"You're damned right. I don't need the hassle, the pain or the long lonely nights in the real afterward."

"In other words—"

He picked up an empty whiskey bottle off the floor and slammed it down on the card table. Keely jumped back. "In other words, when you walk out. When the great sex is no longer enough. When you realize that what you feel is more pity than anything else."

"Pity! For you? You're wrong."

He moved close to her until they stood bare toes to stockinged toes. "What about when Seth told you about me? What about when I told you about Sadie? What about when I told you about Marcie leaving? Why couldn't you have been just great in the sack? Silent and satisfying. Why do you always have to question and probe and analyze?" At the sudden paleness on her cheeks, he swore and stalked away from her.

Keely walked over to a half-full bottle of Jack Daniel's and opened it. She tipped it up to her mouth and drank, coughing, choking and sputtering. Jed quickly crossed the room and jerked the bottle away from her. "Are you crazy?"

"Yes. Slowly going that way. You think I wanted to fall in love with you? I didn't! You weren't my type, remember? It was only chemistry, remember? We could handle it, remember?"

Weary, he put the bottle down and raked his fingers through his hair. "I haven't had any peace since the day I came home and found you in my bed."

"I wasn't technically—" she began.

He glowered at her. "You were in it! And that's where I've wanted you since that afternoon. You with your dreams and your determination. All I wanted to be was the guy who kept the Judge's daughter from getting hurt. I didn't want to feel anything more for you than protectiveness."

Her eyes brightened. "You do feel something more. You just said you do."

"Why don't you just let it go, Keely?"

The brightness changed to a pained look. "Because I can't! Because I'm miserable and lonely and I don't give a damn about any of the things I used to care about." She backed up and sat down on the edge of his bed, folding her arms around her middle.

Jed allowed his eyes to absorb her unhappiness and her vulnerability. This was the other side of the feisty lady with the switchblade he'd come home and found so many weeks ago. He'd managed to prevent her from being hurt by Turk and the others, but what about what he'd done to her? He'd hurt her, and in hurting her, he'd opened himself up to feelings he hadn't believed existed.

He stood in front of her, brushing his hand over her shortened hair. "You look like Peter Pan," he said softly. Her arms came up around his waist and she held him to her, her cheek against the front of his jeans.

The rain continued. The sound of traffic moving down the wet streets drifted in the window. A radio played soft rock. The bed groaned when Jed rested his knee on one corner.

His hand continued to smooth over the crown of her head. "What did the board say?"

He heard her shuddering sigh. Without moving her cheek away from the front of his jeans, she told him their decision.

When she finished, he said, "You don't sound too excited. Isn't that what you wanted?"

"Not nearly as much as I want you."

"You're not gonna drop it, are you?" When she tipped her head back and shook her head, he couldn't stop himself.

He pulled her down on the bed and kissed her. He kissed her hard and long, gathering her taste into his senses. When she fit her body into his, he opened the buttons of her blouse. Her breasts were warm, her lace bra all that separated them from his fingers. He stroked and fanned the lace across her nipples. At her moan, he told himself to stop, but when she unbuttoned his jeans, he made himself stop.

He rolled to a sitting position, took a deep breath and stood up. Rebuttoning his jeans took all his concentration.

He didn't look at her. He didn't dare.

Crossing to the window, he glanced down at the soggy mess of paper. He hunkered down, his fingers picking up a clump and dropping it. "After I left you, after I got drunk enough to do it, I tore up the scrapbook."

Keely lay on her side and watched him. She thought he looked like a man who'd just killed an animal to put it out of its misery.

He glared up at her, his eyes cold, his expression distant. She wanted to tell him he didn't have to tell her, but instead she remained silent, resting her cheek on his pillow.

Swearing softly, he concentrated on a spot above her head. "I kept it because it was a solid reminder that there were people like your father and Sadie, who wanted me. One of the worst moments in my life was when I was about ten years old. I looked in a store window and I realized not one person in the world cared if I lived or died. Until Sadie. Sadie's picture was the first one. A glued-down past . . ." His voice trailed off.

"Oh Jed . . ."

He shook his head at her. "Let me finish. After I met you, watched you at the Island, knew that I wanted you, I kept telling myself it was physical. And when I knew it was more, it scared me. I think I knew it that morning at the diner when I told you I wasn't sleeping with Patsy. That's when I started to let you into my life. The glued-down pictures weren't enough anymore."

While he talked, she slowly got up off the bed and moved over to the wet torn scrapbook. She knelt down beside him and slid her hand over the hard muscle in his thigh.

Her blouse was still unbuttoned. He placed his hand on her left breast and held it there as though counting the beats of her heart.

"When you begged me to make love to you after I ran out of condoms, I was sure the idea of being pregnant with my kid would turn you off. Do you remember what you said?" He glanced up at her, and then away as though he was afraid of her answer.

"That I probably wouldn't be that lucky."

He lowered his head. She heard a soft puff of breath. Relief that she'd remembered? she wondered.

"When you grow up believing no one wants you, and then when you said that—it blew my mind. I kept thinking about it, trying to figure it out."

"There's nothing to figure out. I love you." Keely knew she'd said the words already, but she wanted Jed to believe them. She wanted him to get used to hearing them.

"Can I tell you something?" When he didn't object, she said, "For all Dad did for you, he didn't show you how a man can love a woman. He was wrong to not allow Mom and me to live on the Island. His love for his family, for Mom and for me, should have been part of his work because we were part of him. But he separated it. I know his intentions were good, but they were wrong. We could have learned from the Island and the kids. Instead, Mom spent her time playing bridge and waiting for Dad to come home. I grew up wondering if he loved me."

"He did, babe."

"I know now he did, but I didn't when I was a kid."

He wrapped his arm around her neck. "Knowing you're loved and wanted is important to a kid." He paused. "You scare me, Keely. The scrapbook was easy. Put the pictures in and tell myself that these are the people who wanted me. They were the ones I could be sure of."

"Jed." She combed her hand through the soft silk of his hair. Softly, she whispered, "I was in the scrapbook. Remember?"

He looked at her for a very long time, and then slowly stood. Keely moved with him. She placed her hand on his chest, inside his shirt, over his heart.

His arms came around her, pulling her so tight that she thought he'd never let her go. "You were in the scrapbook," he murmured almost in awe. "All along you were there."

"Yes."

He held on to her, hugging her tighter and tighter. "All along you were there," he repeated. "All along I cared about you and I didn't know it."

"Yes."

They held each other, the rain blowing through the window, wetting them, but neither noticed.

Finally, Jed moved so that he could look at her, at eyes that promised renewal. He'd seen that when she'd first come to ask him to go to the Island. Incredibly, some untapped emotion inside him knew that with Keely Lockwood there was renewal, a chance to let himself go, to allow the fear of rejection to slide away. She said she loved him. Despite all the hell he'd put her through, put himself through, she loved him.

"I love you," he murmured softly, testing the words he'd never said to any woman. They felt brand-new and awkward, but they were real. "I love you."

Keely cried. She couldn't help it, she didn't want to help it. He kissed her eyes, her tears, her cheeks, her mouth. Then after another long hungry kiss that neither one of them could get enough of, he lifted her and carried her to the bed.

"We have to get married," he told her with a grin. He unbuttoned his jeans and helped her out of her clothes.

She laughed, joy bursting through her. He loved her. He loved her!

He lay down beside her and pulled her into his arms, kissing her again. "If I'm going back to the Island with you in September, I intend to sleep with you, not spend every night thinking about it. There's a no-sex rule, remember?"

She pressed closer to him and was rewarded with a groan of satisfaction. She scattered kisses on his throat, his chin, his cheeks and finally his mouth. "That's why you want to marry me? For sex?"

His fingers investigated the shape of her breast. He ducked his head and kissed the rosy nipple, then glanced up at her. His gray eyes were warm, soft. "Not a good enough reason, huh?"

"It's a lousy reason."

"I got a better one."

"I hope so."

"I want to marry you because I love you."

And that, she decided when he rolled on top of her, fitting their bodies together, was the very best reason of all.

*   *   *   *   *

You'll flip . . . your pages won't!
Read paperbacks *hands-free* with

Book Mate • I

The perfect "mate" for all your romance paperbacks
Traveling • Vacationing • At Work • In Bed • Studying
• Cooking • Eating

Perfect size for all standard paperbacks, this wonderful invention makes reading a pure pleasure! Ingenious design holds paperback books OPEN and FLAT so even wind can't ruffle pages — leaves your hands free to do other things. Reinforced, wipe-clean vinyl-covered holder flexes to let you turn pages without undoing the strap . . . supports paperbacks so well, they have the strength of hardcovers!

Pages turn WITHOUT opening the strap.

SEE-THROUGH STRAP

Reinforced back stays flat

Built in bookmark

BOOK MARK

BACK COVER HOLDING STRIP

10" x 7¼" opened.
Snaps closed for easy carrying, too